TEMPTING THE ARTIST

SHARON C. COOPER

Bestselling author Sharon C. Cooper brings you another exciting romance…

Tempting the Artist, book 3 of the Jenkins Family Series:

Christina "CJ" Jenkins, a free-spirited painter by trade is juggling her obligation to the family construction business, with the demands of her secret passion. A secret life she has successfully hidden until recently. When sexy, bad-boy attorney, Luke Hayden, enters the picture, he steals her heart. But the truth of Christina's double life buried under lies, threatens to destroy them both.

Luke is leaving New York to escape the drama, which is his life. Starting over in Cincinnati with Christina appeals to him more than he will admit. Although her secret jeopardizes their steamy affair, it's not until someone threatens to destroy the Jenkins family empire, and uses Luke to carry out their plan, that their relationship is truly tested. Luke will do what he can to help the Jenkins family, but he will stop at nothing to tempt the woman who has captured his heart.

CHAPTER ONE

Christina Jenkins folded her lower lip between her teeth, her hands on her hips as she paced in front of the wall of windows that overlooked Central Park East. The landmark view was of no use to her as she debated on what she should do about Luke Hayden. The man had captured her heart, tempting her to share a secret that she hadn't even shared with her family.

I need to tell him.

I have to tell him.

She released a quiet groan and ran tense hands through a mass of curly hair. Frustration lodged in her chest. Christina knew she could have handled this a month ago. Instead, she waited until the last possible moment, and now she was starting to get on her own nerves with worry.

It was almost midnight. Well past the time she should have been asleep since they had to get up early in the morning. Well, actually she didn't have to get up. She wouldn't be on the 8 a.m. flight to Cincinnati.

Leaning against the window frame, she contemplated her next move. *What am I going to do?* At some point, she would have to tell Luke she wasn't traveling with him. He was leaving the big city of dreams and relocating to her hometown of Cincinnati.

Her gaze drifted to the twinkling city lights and the skyscrapers that were too close together, but made up the city she had fallen in love with. Why would he leave all of this? Luke had told her that he'd had enough of New York's fast pace. She wasn't buying it. No one left New York City for Cincinnati, Ohio. Granted she liked living in Cincinnati, but she loved the energy of The Big Apple.

Maybe he's hiding something. That had to be it. Yet who was she to question his decision or his secrets, especially when she had a secret of her own.

She stepped away from the spectacular view and leaned on the back of a white chaise lounge, one of two pieces of furniture that hadn't been picked up by the movers. Luke had sold everything else except a few items remaining in the living room and his bedroom set. The young couple, who bought the apartment, had worked the remaining pieces into their purchase offer.

Christina lowered her head and shut her eyes. Everything would be all right. She was overthinking the situation. Their relationship was tight and built on trust. Besides, Luke was the sweetest man she had ever met, and he wouldn't have a problem with her change in plans. It wasn't like she wasn't ever going back to Cincinnati. She was only staying in New York another day, two tops.

"You've been on edge all night."

Christina's head jerked up startled at the sound of Luke's voice. Her heart pounded erratically in her chest. She wasn't sure if it was because of the conversation she knew they had to have or because she hadn't heard him enter the room. After an amazing round of sex, she had left him sleeping in the bedroom while she hung out in the living room weighing her options.

Luke stepped out of the shadows of the semi-dark room and into a small stream of moonlight shining through one of the windows. After three months of dating, the sight of him still made her heart stutter.

Absolute perfection.

She had always been attracted to dark skinned men, a stark contrast to her lighter skin. And this man was the epitome of sexy. He stood before her in nothing but a pair of striped pajama bottoms hanging low on his hips, his thick package pressed behind the flimsy material. Her gaze moved up to his face. An artist would be in heaven if they had him as a model. Sharp accessing eyes, an average-size nose and a chiseled jaw line made up his handsome face. And those lips. God, the things he could do with those full, tempting lips.

Lust throbbed through Christina's veins as Luke watched her with the intensity of a hawk circling its target calculating the perfect time to pounce. The dress shirt she wore of his, with nothing underneath, did nothing to hide her erect nipples from his heated gaze. All it took was a look from him, and she was ready to let him have his way with her. Again.

"Wha ... what are you doing up?" she finally asked.

"I don't sleep well without you in my bed." His slumber-filled voice was deep and intoxicating. She had no doubt that he meant what he said. When she wasn't in New York visiting him, he rarely slept in the bed, preferring the sofa in his home office. He'd often stay at work until nine or ten at night, only to arrive home and work for another few hours. She had no idea how he functioned with only three or four hours of sleep each night.

Luke moved across the room with the stealth of a lion, closing in on its prey. With a lean body, his sculpted chest and muscular biceps stood out. That quiet control swimming in his eyes, with a twinge of fearlessness, rooted her in place and had her heart pounding double-time. She was sure that look played well into him being one of the top defense attorneys at his New York law firm.

"What's wrong? You've been distracted since we

returned from the art show." The richness of his baritone voice washed over her like a smooth, satiny caress. And he smelled so good. The fresh scent of soap permeated the air as if he had just stepped out of the shower. His voice, his scent, and all that made him the man he was, weakened her defenses and sent her senses spiraling out of control.

He pulled her effortlessly against his hard body and her arms slid easily around his neck. What she felt for him was unlike anything she had ever experienced. There was just something about him. Something about the way his welcoming embrace evoked a sense of peace that settled over her like a goose down jacket all snuggly and warm. And there was something about the way his self-assuredness gave her the desire to experience the world through his eyes, making her want to try new things and live life on the edge.

Christina moaned as his body molded against hers, chest to chest and thigh to thigh. He felt too good. It wasn't helping that the feathery kisses he placed along the length of her neck were reigniting the smoldering heat from hours earlier. She couldn't think straight. Couldn't think straight when he looked at her, or when he kissed her, or when he touched her. An experienced lover, his caress had her body bending to his will.

"Maybe you should come back to bed so that I can make you forget your troubles."

"Or maybe you can make me forget my troubles right here … right now."

"That can be arranged." She leaned against the back of the chair as his fingers quickly undid the buttons on her shirt. The expensive material slid off her shoulders and down her arms. "You looked good in my shirt, but you'd look even better out of it." Luke tossed the garment to the side, letting it fall to the floor.

Christina had always been comfortable in the nude, and watching Luke's appreciative gaze travel down the length of her body made her glad she'd only worn his shirt.

Nudging her legs apart, he stepped between her thighs and a shiver of delight shot through her when his hand flattened over her breast. With her arms behind her, she held on to the back of the chair for support as he caressed, squeezed, and tweaked a taut nipple. Holding her around her waist, he lowered his head, and his tongue took over where his fingers left off. Lethal. That's what she considered his tongue to be. Her insides turned to mush when his mouth made contact with her body.

She moaned when he paid her other nipple the same homage as the first, gently taking it between his teeth. His hands caressed the curve of her torso and worked their way down to her hips. Heart pounding erratically, Christina squirmed beneath him. Wanting more. Needing more. Savoring the way his lower body ground against her nakedness.

His mouth returned to her lips, and he kissed her with a hunger that radiated to the soles of her feet. When his large hands gripped her bare butt cheeks, she wrapped her arms around his neck, pulling him closer, his erection pressing against her stomach. She gave herself completely to the passion of his kiss. Her body was coming alive with every stroke of his tongue and squeeze of his hand.

"Damn, baby you feel good," he mumbled against her lips. "But I need to feel all of you." His right hand slid between their bodies, and he loosened the drawstring of his pajamas.

Oh yes. Her body pulsed with anticipation, anxious to have him inside of her. But suddenly she realized what they were about to do.

No. No. No. What am I thinking? I can't do this. I have to tell him.

Breathing hard, she snatched her mouth from his. "Wait." She wiggled beneath him. "I have to tell you something." He stiffened in her hold. A shiver scurried down her spine as his piercing eyes searched hers. "We need to talk."

"Now?" he croaked, his eyes narrowed and his breath came in short spurts.

She nodded.

Luke released a frustrated groan and lowered his head to her shoulder. Dropping his hands from her body, he grabbed hold of the back of the chair, locking her between his arms. He breathed in and out several times before slowly lifting his head.

"You do know those four words are a mood killer right?" His deep voice still held a hint of sleepiness, but his eyes were alert and as penetrating as usual.

When Christina didn't respond, he lifted up and adjusted himself, tightening the drawstring of his pajama bottoms. She knew she should have stopped him before it went this far, but how could she? His lips and hands were magical, capable of clouding her mind.

He handed her the shirt that he had just helped her out of and stood staring as she slipped her arms into the sleeves. A mixture of emotions tumbled in her gut and her hand rested against her chest as if that could help her breathe and steady her pounding heart. If he wasn't disappointed in her for putting on the brakes with what almost just happened, he was sure to be pissed at her after they talked.

Luke blew out another breath and grabbed her hand, leading her to the only other furniture left in the living room, a sofa.

They sat next to each other, and he stretched his long legs out in front him, his head resting against the back of the furniture. "All right talk to me. What's going on?" He turned his head slightly to look at her. "Did something happen while we were at the gallery?"

Earlier they had attended an art show featuring Sasha Knight's work, Christina's favorite artist. She had thought about coming clean with Luke while there, especially since the show was her main reason for wanting to stay in New York for another day or two.

Just tell him.

"I'm not flying back to Cincinnati with you in the morning. I've decided to stay in New York for another day."

He studied her for the longest, not speaking. Tension bounced off him like hail against a tin roof, and Christina braced herself for an argument. Their relationship was perfect, but springing this on him after a month of planning, probably wasn't going to go as well as she hoped.

He stood and eased over to the corner fireplace, rubbing the top of his head with one hand, and the other on his hip. "You've decided to stay?" He turned back to her and leaned against the marble surrounding the fireplace, his muscular arms now folded across his broad chest.

This was a good sign. He appeared calm, yet the tension between them could still be felt even ten feet away.

"I know I probably should have said something sooner, but I want to stay until the end of Sasha Knight's show. I know we saw most of her new work, but I heard there would be some new pieces on display tomorrow."

"Are you kidding me?" His voice rose with each word. "You have several of her paintings and have attended every one of her shows. Why the hell do you need to stay longer? And why didn't you tell me sooner? We've had this weekend's travel planned for over a month."

"Luke, calm down." She stood, but maintained her position near the sofa.

"I am calm, dammit!"

"No, you're not. You're trying to start an argument."

"I'm a lawyer, Christina. Arguing is what I do, especially when someone is withholding facts from me or screwing me around."

"I'm not trying to screw you around. I'm just saying—"

"Stop!" He lifted his hand and glared at her. "I want to make sure I have this correct. My woman who came to New York to see me and help me finish packing, suddenly tells me that she's not traveling with me. The same woman who I have had countless conversations with regarding the move, as well as the travel arrangements. And you're telling me I should be calm about this bit of information that you're *just* springing on me?"

"Yes, but—"

"What the hell am I supposed to think, CJ?" She stood rooted in place as he slowly approached her. "You know me well enough to know that I don't like half-truths. So if that's what you're giving me here, you need to come clean now. I'm leaving New York to get away from the bullshit. I'm not trying to take on more bullshit."

Instead of answering his questions or commenting, she remained silent. She had a good reason for wanting to stay. She just wasn't ready to share that reason with him or anyone else for that matter. Yes, she knew he didn't play games, and she also knew how he felt about trust and honesty. He had never gone into great detail, but she sensed that he'd trusted the wrong person in the past and had been hurt.

"Can't you just accept that I'd like to stay for another day or two? I'll be in Cincinnati before you know it. What's the big deal?"

Why'd she say that? His harsh laugh sent a chill down her spine. He was around six feet tall, but it was as if he grew several inches instantly. This was probably the Luke Hayden, who showed up to court every week. This was the attorney who had never lost a case, and this was the attorney who was a force to be reckoned with.

"What's the big deal?" he mocked her, his voice low and menacing. "The big deal is that you waited until the last possible minute to tell me as if you're hiding something. I'm sure the desire to stay a day or two longer didn't just pop into your head tonight, and besides that, you're making a fool of me. Here I thought you've been coming to New York to see me, when it's clear there's something else going on. And before you say anything, I'm not buying that you're that in love with Sasha Knight's work." Silence circled them as his dark, penetrating gaze bore into her with the intensity of a masonry drill bit through a concrete wall. "Is it someone else?"

"No!" She rushed to him, her hands on his rock-hard torso. "Baby, no. There's no one else. I swear to you." How could he even think she would be involved with someone else? Sure, she might be evading his questions, and sure she wanted to stay in New York a little longer. But there was no way she was interested in anyone else.

He stepped out of her grasp. "Then you need to tell me what's going on."

"Luke." She reached out to him, but he took another step back as if her touch caused him pain. "Let's not do this. I don't want our wonderful night to end like this."

"Then tell me what the hell is going on." Apparently, she hesitated too long. He raised his hands. "Never mind. I've dealt with enough lies from others to last me a lifetime. I don't need them from you too." He turned away and headed to his bedroom, but stopped, his back to her, his hands gripping each side of the doorjamb. "You might not be planning to leave New York anytime soon, but have your shi... You'll need to be out of here by six a.m."

Christina startled when he slammed the door behind him. *Why couldn't I just tell him?*

CHAPTER TWO

Three Months Later

Luke Hayden rocked in the high-back office chair and tapped his pen against the top of the mahogany desk. Three months and two weeks to the day, he had landed in Cincinnati, Ohio, and immediately started a new life at the law offices of Atwater, Rouse & Stevenson. To say they operated differently than the law firm he'd left in New York would be an understatement.

He pushed away from the desk and walked across the office to the coffee pot. "I definitely got what I asked for," he mumbled to himself. A slower, calmer environment, which didn't include eighty-hour work weeks was different. Yet, the jury was still out on whether or not the move had been a good one. Initially, he couldn't wait to get to Cincinnati and start anew. Not only because it was past time for him to leave New York, but also because he thought he and Christina had the start of something good.

She had called him three times since he'd arrived in Cincinnati and three times he let those calls go to voicemail. She might have been right that they needed to talk, but despite missing her like crazy, he couldn't do it. He couldn't allow her any more space in his head, or in his heart. The problem was, there wasn't a day that went by that he didn't think about Christina. Maybe he should have been more understanding of her change of plans back then, anything to keep what he thought they were building together. But he had been jerked around enough in court by opposing counsels. No way was he going to let a woman make a fool of him or play with his heart.

He poured a cup of coffee and raised the mug to his lips, but stopped midway when someone knocked on his office door. Before he could answer, the door swung open.

Gary Rouse stepped into Luke's office as if he had been invited. "When do you want to meet on the Goss case?" He held up a thick folder and dropped down onto the upholstered chair in front of Luke's desk, crossing one ankle over his knee.

Repulsion simmered in Luke's gut at the sight of Rouse, and he gripped his coffee mug tighter. Slimeball. Stupid Jerk. Asshole. All names that Luke used to refer to his archenemy. Up for a partnership, Gary's claws came out the moment Luke took up space in one of the corner offices. Anthony Rouse, a senior partner who happened to be Gary's father, had informed Luke that the office setup was temporary, until they made some internal changes. Apparently the changes hadn't been made. Luke still had the office. But from day one, Gary saw the setup as Luke moving in on his territory. Little did Gary know, Luke wasn't interested in a partnership.

Been there, done that.

Luke walked back to his desk and set the coffee mug down, still not responding. He didn't like Gary. A slick talker to the nth degree and a royal pain in Luke's ass, it was taking Herculean strength not to tell his fellow attorney what he could do with his cases. But Luke also knew oh too well that anxious feeling an attorney gets when he or she is up for partner. The desire to be the best and win every case to snag the partnership. He remembered the feeling prior to becoming a senior partner. But it wasn't until those last months in New York that he felt the weight of the responsibility. That last case made him realize the man he had become. A man he didn't like.

"You can check with Robin in the morning and find out when I have an opening this week." Luke reclaimed his seat. He could easily check his schedule to determine a good time to meet, but why should he? Gary was the one who needed his assistance, not the other way around. From day one, the guy treated Luke as if he were a paralegal or some first-year law student. They both knew that Luke had enough past experiences and successes to replace any one of the senior partners at Atwater, Rouse & Stevenson.

"I just want to know. Who goes from being a high profile New York City defense attorney to a construction litigator in Cincinnati, Ohio?"

Damn. Not this shit again. Luke gripped the edge of his desk. A scathing retort teetered on the tip of his tongue. If he had to have this conversation with Gary one more time, he was going to be the one needing a defense attorney. He wanted more than anything to tell the pompous jerk where he could go, but there was no sense in making the growing tension between them any worse.

"Is there something else you need Attorney Rouse?" Luke leaned back in his office chair and stared the man down. The guy was a punk. It was no wonder he'd been there for seven years and still hadn't made partner. "Because if there isn't, you can show yourself out of my office."

Gary glanced back at the closed door before he leaned forward in his seat. "Yeah, there is something else. I need you to pack your shit and find somewhere else to practice law. We don't need you coming in here trying to make the rest of us look bad just because you've practice at a big-time firm in New York."

Luke studied the man who was around his same age, thirty-five, yet there were days when his nemesis acted as if he was still in high school. Short with an athletic build, Gary flirted with all of the secretaries, came to work late, and most days left before everyone else. It didn't help that his father coddled him. Despite all of that though, Gary was old enough and should have been wise enough to know when it was a bad idea to step to another grown-ass man with some bullshit.

Luke stood slowly, his pulse pounding in his ear. He had never been very good at holding his temper when dealing with an adversary, but years of defending some of the country's most dangerous people had taught him how to tread lightly.

Gary also stood. His height inferior to Luke's. Wariness swam in his eyes, and he jerked back when Luke placed his palms faced down on top of his desk.

"Don't let this suit fool you, asshole." Luke's voice was low and lethal, reminiscent to a stealth bomb designed to seek and destroy. "I have worked my butt off for the last ten years keeping my clients out of jail – some not guilty, but most guilty of the crimes which they had been accused. Don't think I don't know how to get away with murder." He let his words sink in as he stared Gary down. "Now get the hell out of my office."

The scowl on the man's face let Luke know that this wasn't the last confrontation they'd have.

The moment the door closed behind Gary, Luke's cell phone rang. Wound tighter than a perp being hauled off to jail, he debated on whether or not to let the call go to voicemail before finally answering.

"Hello."

"Dang man, they working you too hard or something? You sound like you're about ready to kick some tail."

Luke rubbed his forehead and chuckled. A moment ago, he almost lost his mind and did just that, not caring that he would have been out on his ass and looking for a lawyer to defend him.

"Well, well, well, if it isn't Zachary Anderson, my long lost friend."

Zack laughed. "You act as if we haven't talked in years. It's been what, a few weeks?" Luke smiled at hearing his best friend's voice. There was one advantage to moving to Cincinnati; he got a chance to hang out with a few of his longtime friends.

"More like a month. So I take it you're back in the city."

"Yes sir, and I'm calling to see if you want to hook up for a drink after work?"

"What, you have a job now?" Luke joked. Zack, a former NFL star running back for the Cincinnati Cougars, had retired months earlier.

"Oh, so you have jokes. I'll have you know that I have a full-time job, and that's catering to my beautiful wife's every desire."

Luke shook his head. "Man, I can't believe how Jada has you wrapped around her perfectly manicured finger. It saddens me to watch how the mighty have fallen." They laughed, but Luke's chest tightened at the mention of Jada. Hearing her name always made him think of Christina, Jada's cousin.

"Don't hate man. This is going to be you one day."

"I don't know about all of that, but on a serious note, I'm happy for you."

They caught up for a few minutes before agreeing to meet at a nearby bar later that evening. Luke needed some fun. Other than showing up at the office each day, he hadn't been out and about the way he would've been in New York. Granted Cincinnati didn't offer the number of activities and restaurants as New York, but it was home. His new home.

An hour later, Luke strolled into the bar and glanced around the semi-crowded space searching for Zack. He spotted him at the bar signing an autograph. The pimple-faced fan was grinning so hard; one would think Zack was the President of the United States.

Some things never changed, retired or not.

Since Zack's first year in the National Football League, it had been the same scene. He drew fans the way bees swarmed to honey and never let the fame go to his head. The guy was the real deal. The nicest person one could ever meet and generous to a fault.

"I see you're still the superstar," Luke said when the fan walked away. "Are you sure you have time to hang out with us little people?"

Zack glanced up and grinned. "Yeah right, like you're one of the little people. I'm sure you're still fielding offers from the top New York firms, trying to entice you back to the east coast." He stood and grabbed hold of Luke's outstretched hand, pulling him in for a one-arm hug. "Long time no see, man." They pounded each other on the back." Zack reclaimed his seat at the bar, and Luke sat next to him. "Glad you were able to make it. So, whatcha drinkin'?"

"Scotch."

"That kind of day, huh?" Zack gave the bartender the order and ordered himself another beer.

"Yeah, something like that." Actually, his day was fine until Gary walked into his office. Luke was still kicking himself for the way he handled the situation. He said what needed to be said to Gary, but Luke knew he could have come up with a more diplomatic way of telling the jerk to go and screw himself.

"So what's been going on?" Luke asked just as the bartender set his drink in front of him.

"Not too much. Last week Jada and I were in California hanging out for a few days and then we flew to Connecticut where I met with ESPN. We've been talking back and forth about me guest hosting some of the shows during this coming football season."

"Ah, man, that's cool. Who knows, maybe the

opportunity will turn into something permanent."

Zack took a swig of his Bud Light. "Nah, I'm not looking for a full-time job or anything permanent. It'll be cool to guest host a few times, but that'll be enough."

Luke looked at his friend's profile. "Considering how happy you appear, I assume marriage is agreeing with you." Zack's deep tan and the blond streaks highlighting his hair was a sure sign that he had gotten a lot of sun while out in California. Luke thought back to when they were in college and how the going joke was that Zack wasn't really white, but a black man with light skin. He grew up around African Americans in a rough area of Columbus, Ohio and at times even sounded like them. Zack was one of the people Luke had befriended during undergrad, and they'd been best of friends ever since. "You're looking good man. Retirement agrees with you. And the beard. You have the whole retirement-look thing going on."

Zack chuckled and rubbed the short hairs on his chin. "Life is good man. Marriage is great. Jada is the best thing that has ever happened to me."

"Well, that's saying a lot considering you're a former NFL star running back, a multi-millionaire, and you have more endorsement deals than most football retirees. Who knew it could get any better than that?"

"I know, right? I'm blessed, man. Playing in the league for so many years doing something I absolutely loved was more than I could ask for, but then I met Jada." He shook his head and smiled as if thinking about a specific moment. "Our marriage has exceeded my expectations."

A pang of longing lodged in Luke's chest as he listened to Zack talk about how great marriage was. He had never even entertained the thought of spending the rest of his life in a committed relationship until Christina had come along. With that ended, he had no intention of ever allowing a woman to get that close to his heart again.

"It seems as if I've known Jada forever. I knew the type

of woman I wanted, but she's so much more."

"I guess when it's right, its right." Luke was glad someone was happy in their relationship. He knew of very few people who could say the same.

"But enough about me. What's going on with you? How's the new firm?"

Luke filled him in on the slower pace and the lighter workload. Speaking about his new job aloud, Luke had to admit that he definitely got what he had hoped for as it related to shorter work weeks and less stress. What he hadn't counted on was the lack of challenge that came with joining the new firm. He had no doubt that if he had gone in for a health screening months ago, his blood pressure would have been in the danger zone. Whereas lately, his cases didn't get a rise out of him. He also told Zack about his dealings with Gary.

Zack shook his head and laughed. "You're probably the only person I know who is brave enough to threaten another attorney *and* in a law office."

"Yeah, I lost my head for a moment there. Every time the guy steps into my office and opens his mouth, I want to shove my fist into it. I guess this afternoon could've been worse. I could've punched him and then threatened him."

"Yeah, do that and you'll be the one needing an attorney. Knowing the hooligan you were back in college, it's almost comical that you're a lawyer."

Luke had to smile. Looking back at some of their run-ins after a night of partying, he was glad they lived to tell about them. It had taken him a while to settle down even after becoming a lawyer. Passionate about defending his clients, he recalled a number of arguments with other attorneys. Cursing them out when they talked crap or withheld information.

"I guess I should put some bail money aside for you, just in case." They both laughed.

"Trust me. I'm not trying to end up in court, or going

before the ABA because I kicked a fellow lawyer's ass."

Zack looked at Luke sideways. Luke knew his friend wanted to say more, so he waited. He really wasn't in the mood to talk, especially about himself, but they hadn't had a lengthy conversation in months.

"What about that other situation?" Zack finally asked. "I trust none of that drama followed you here."

Now this was a subject he didn't want to discuss. Outside of his colleagues at the New York law firm, Zack was the only person who knew about the troubles with Luke's last case and how the incident could have cost Luke his life.

Luke threw back the last of his Scotch and signaled the bartender over. "Nah. Everything's cool." Zack didn't want anything else, and though Luke didn't want another Scotch, he knew he'd need at least a beer or two. "I'll stay put in Cincinnati for a few years until I decide my next step."

"Speaking of next step, you never gave me details about what happened between you and CJ. You guys were going pretty hot and heavy. What went wrong?"

Luke shook his head. "Things fell apart so fast, I barely know what happened." Luke told Zack about his last night in New York. Talking about the breakup made him relive the disappointment, anger, and frustration of that night. He thought for sure Christina would have been a distant memory by now.

"I asked her if she was seeing someone else and she said no. But what else could it have been?"

Zack shook his head. "I don't know what that was all about, but I know CJ. She's not the two-timing type. I also know that when you find someone special, you don't give up without a fight. If she's the one or even if you think she's the one, don't let her go."

"She's already gone," Luke said dryly. "I'm done. It's over. I've moved on, and I'm sure she has too."

Zack swiveled on the bar stool, to face Luke. "I don't know this for sure, but I don't think she's gone, as you say. I think she's doing what you're doing, trying to move on, but not because she wants to."

Luke sat up straight, giving Zack his full attention. "So exactly what do you know? Not that I'm trying to get back with her."

Zack grinned. "Yeah, sure. All I'm going to say is that you owe it to the both of you to at least know the facts. All of the facts before you totally walk away."

Shaking his head, Luke turned back to face the bar. "I don't know if I can handle seeing her again." He knew he sounded like a punk. But when he woke up that next morning in New York, after their argument, to find Christina gone, he knew she had taken a part of his heart with her.

"Are you sure you've moved on? Have you been out with anyone since relocating here?"

He hadn't gone out with anyone, but it wasn't for lack of offers. The women in Cincinnati were just as bold as the ones in New York. He'd turned down a number of invites for a drink or dinner.

"I'll take your silence and that far-away look in your eye as a 'no' to both questions."

"Christina and I are history," he reiterated. He wasn't sure if the words were spoken for Zack's benefit or his.

Zack took a swig from the beer he'd been nursing. "As far as I know, CJ isn't seeing anyone. As a matter of fact, she's probably still trying to get settled."

"What do you mean settled?"

"I sold her my loft."

Luke narrowed his eyes. "The one a few blocks from here?"

Zack nodded.

"How the hell could she afford something like that on her salary? She still working for her family's construction company?"

Zack nodded again. "Yeah, she's still there. I guess she's a good saver. Because though I gave her a serious deal, I was a little surprised that she was able to swing the price."

Luke dissected that bit of information. Christina didn't splurge on clothes, handbags and any of the other things women loved spending money on. Yet, earning forty or forty-five thousand a year as a house painter wouldn't get her into a million dollar loft.

"So if you had another chance with her, would you take it?" Zack interrupted Luke's thoughts. "'Cause I know you still care about her."

Would he give it another shot if an opportunity presented itself? "I don't know. I've been here for months and haven't run into her. I don't see our paths crossing."

"You could always call her. I'm just sayin'." When Luke didn't respond, Zack continued. "Well, whatever you end up doing, just know you're not the only one who has had to deal with a Jenkins woman. It's not easy, man, but it's worth it. I'll have to let you know when Craig, Toni's husband, starts that support group."

Luke frowned. "What support group?"

"A support group for any man married to or dealing with a Jenkins woman." Luke chuckled and bumped his beer bottle to Zack's in a toast.

"Let me know when and where the first meeting is being held."

They hung out for another hour, and Luke realized how much he had missed his old college buddy. He was also reminded that he needed to get a life.

Luke walked the short distance to what was quickly becoming his favorite hamburger joint in Mt. Adams. Not because the food was all that great, but because it was near his condominium and the service was fast.

He reached into his pocket for a pack of cigarettes. He had been trying to stop smoking for over six months, and though the nicotine craving was fading, he hadn't totally won the battle. His mind immediately went to Christina. While they were together, he had come close, only having one or two cigarettes a day. Once they parted ways, so did his will power to quit.

Stopping a few feet from the entrance to the restaurant, Luke lit a cigarette. That first puff always relaxed him. Not that he was stressed, but there was something about the smoothness of the smoke when he'd inhale, that brought a certain peace.

Leaning against the brick of the building, he took in his surroundings. At nine o'clock at night, the area was still lively with twenty and thirty year olds bar hopping. But it was nothing like New York. He had to admit, there were some aspects of New York that he did miss. The bustling sidewalks, the Broadway shows, and the food. God he missed the food. New York had some of the best restaurants in the world, and it would be worth a trip back for a slice of real pizza.

Yeah, he missed those things but gone were stressful cases, sleepless nights, and cray-cray clients. Those things alone made the move worthwhile.

Luke took a long drag from his cigarette and almost choked on the smoke when he glanced up the street. He'd know that sexy walk anywhere. The bounce of her hair, the gentle sway of her hips from left to right, and that long stride that made her look as if she were gliding instead of walking.

Christina.

What were the chances of him running into her, especially roaming around this time of night? In all the time of living in Cincinnati, he hadn't seen her. At first, he had been glad. Seeing her would bring back memories, and he didn't want thoughts of her to distract him from starting his new life. But it hadn't work.

He knew the moment she saw him. She missed a step and almost dropped the paper bag she was carrying. She slowed, and her mouth dropped open, but she quickly closed it.

Still beautiful.

All the Jenkins women were gorgeous, but it was

Christina who had captured Luke's attention from the moment they met. He had never believed in love at first sight, but that was exactly what he felt when he saw her at Zack's birthday party months ago. Even now, his pulse pounded, and his body stirred with passion at the sight of her.

Picking up dinner all but forgotten, his gaze took her in. Her head full of curls hanging well past her shoulders were unruly as usual. Just the way he liked them. He could still remember how soft they were to his touch, and he couldn't help but notice her attire or lack of. She was one of those women who believed in being comfortable in whatever she wore. And the fewer the clothes the better, especially when it came to wearing a bra ... or not.

Damn.

The multi-color T-shirt only emphasized the fact that she was braless. Her firm, more-than-a-handful breasts dangled freely behind the thin material, and of course, his body reacted immediately. Those baggy cargo pants that he never liked might have fooled some, but he knew what lay underneath. A tight ass and hips that had just the right amount of curve, which had brought him more pleasure than any man deserved.

She stopped two feet away, and they stared at each other, neither saying a word. Luke could look at her forever and not get tired. Her exotic eyes with naturally long eyelashes had brought him to his knees plenty of times. His gaze took in her perfect nose now sporting a small diamond stud nose-ring that enhanced her sexiness. And those lips. Good Lord. Those full, luscious, tempting ...

Damn. Why the hell was he torturing himself? Upon seeing her, he should have nodded a greeting and headed in the opposite direction. He also should still be angry with her for the way things ended between them. Heck, he should just walk away and pretend he never saw her. But he couldn't. Like smoking, there was an insatiable draw. She was an addiction he couldn't quit.

"You look good." The words tumbled out of his mouth before he could stop them. No hello, no how are you, and no I've missed you like hell. Instead, he said the first thing that popped into his head.

Real brilliant, Counselor.

CHAPTER THREE

"Uh, thanks," Christina said, totally caught off guard. At first, she thought her eyes were playing tricks on her, especially since she had been thinking about Luke only moments earlier. Thoughts of him had plagued her mind every day since returning from New York. If only she could take back that night or get a do-over. There were so many things she would do differently.

"Hi."

The one word seemed so insufficient, but it was the only word Christina could form at the moment. Seeing him, the light scruff on his jaws and chin making him look sexier than she remembered, seemed surreal. When she was walking toward him, he had checked her out from the top of her head to the flip flops on her feet. Now his penetrating eyes studied her face as if seeing her for the first time.

"Hi," he finally said. His dark eyes narrowed as he took a long drag on his cigarette and blew the thin cloud of smoke away from her. His gaze never wavered.

She hated to see he was still smoking, but damn if he didn't look sexy doing it. He had been trying to quit for the longest and was doing so well before they broke up.

"I thought you were quitting." She nodded toward the cigarette between his fingers.

"I am."

She waited, thinking that he'd say more. *Oookay.* Silence stretched between them, and he took two more puffs before snuffing his cigarette out against the brick wall behind him.

"So how have you been?"

Terrible without you in my life is what she wanted to say, but instead she said, "I've been okay. With the summer quickly approaching, things have been pretty busy at work." She had been assigned the lead on one of their larger projects, making her days longer and busier than usual. "How are things with you? Are you all settled in?"

"I'm getting there. For the most part, I've settled in. Still trying to get acclimated at the firm." He shrugged. "But I know it'll take time."

He pushed away from the building and shoved his left hand into his front pants pocket. Of course, her gaze followed his every move, appreciating how good he looked in his blue pinstripe suit with a light-blue shirt and a designer tie knotted perfectly. Most people would've rushed home to relieve themselves of the confining material, but not him. That late at night, he was still dressed in one of his ridiculously priced suits looking like a walking marketing campaign for Armani. He definitely looked out of place.

That area near downtown typically attracted the hipster, free spirited type who wore colorful, baggy clothing, and sometimes clothes with holes in them. And then there was Luke. He looked as if he should be making deals on Wall Street. But then again, there was a side of him that most people didn't get to see. A conundrum, the sexy bad-boy who grew up in Harlem could freestyle the lyrics to a 2 Chainz song and then turn around and passionately discuss the latest Senate bill. One of many aspects about him, which fascinated her.

Say something.

They never had trouble communicating. So his silence was unnerving. Maybe he was still angry with her, but she wished he would yell, curse her out or something. Anything to get a conversation going.

Christina shifted the paper bag in her arms. They needed to talk about what happened in New York. Or at least she wanted them to talk about that night.

"I take it you were able to find an apartment," she said, assuming he was waiting for her to get a conversation started.

"Yeah, a condo about a quarter of a mile that way." He gestured with his thumb in the opposite direction in which she lived. She was surprised to learn that they lived so close to each other. "I heard you purchased Zack's old loft. Impressive."

She shrugged. "Don't be too impressed. He gave me an unbelievable deal." Christina knew Zack could have easily gotten a cool mil for the place.

Christina fidgeted under Luke's scrutiny. She always felt as if his dark eyes could see into her soul. But if that were the case, he'd know how much she missed him and how she regretted the way things ended.

"It's good seeing you again."

"Yeah, you too."

She self-consciously rubbed the back of her neck, her fingers tangling in her hair. She wanted so bad to ask him why he hadn't returned any of her calls. Yet, she kept her mouth closed. She had hurt him. Why would he call?

Christina couldn't take it anymore. The uncomfortable silence was just that, uncomfortable.

"Well, I'd better get going. Take care." She forced her feet to move and started to walk around him. What she really wanted to do was pull his face to hers and taste the lips that were just as tempting as they used to be. She couldn't. She wouldn't put herself through that torture. Besides, one kiss would never be enough.

His brows drew together, but she kept moving, now anxious to get away from him. He touched her arm. "What are you doing walking alone this late at night?"

She glanced down at his hand on her arm, trying like crazy not to show how much his touch affected her. Following her gaze, he quickly released her.

Hurt lodged in her gut. Luke had always been a touchy feely person when it came to her. Even after they had broken up, she had held out hope that they would find their way back to each other. Now it seemed as if that would never happen. He didn't even want to touch her.

Hiding her disappointment, she backed away and forced a smile to her lips. "I needed some air and wanted a snack," she lifted the paper bag of chips and cookies, "and it's a nice night. Besides, I only live a couple of blocks—"

"CJ, we've talked about you walking alone at night. It's not safe."

Was that concern she heard? Was it possible that he still cared?

"That was in New York." She loved walking along Fifth Avenue in Manhattan at all times of the day, window-shopping, and people watching while Luke was at work. He hated it. He didn't care that there was usually a ton of people out and about. He never wanted her walking alone.

He moved closer to her and she swallowed hard. His sexy, confident swagger always turned her on. Tonight was no different.

"It's not safe for you to walk this time of night alone, anywhere." He reached for her small bag of food, cradling it in his left arm while his right hand landed at the small of her back, nudging her in the direction of her loft.

They had made it a half a block before he dropped his hand from her back. Immediately she missed the warmth she hadn't felt in months. They walked in silence. She wanted so bad to beg for his forgiveness and ask for another chance, but he didn't forgive easy. He had lost so much over the years. His mother had died when he was ten and his father, former military who eventually became a cop, had died in the line of duty the same year Luke graduated from law school. Besides some close friends who were like brothers, he was alone.

"Though it's not necessary, thanks for walking with me."

"It's not a problem. I just wish you would take heed to my numerous warnings. We might not be together, but I still care about your safety."

"I appreciate your concern."

"But let me guess, you're going to keep doing it," he said in resignation.

A smile lifted the corners of her mouth. Apparently, he remembered how stubborn she could be. She couldn't help herself. It was in her genes. All the Jenkins women were stubborn.

They continued walking in silence. When two guys, who looked as if they had had a few drinks staggered up the street toward them, Luke moved closer to her. His hand went automatically to the small of her back, pulling her closer. Christina's pulse kicked up. It took everything she had not to wrap her arm around his waist and never let go. Instead, she molded against his side, loving the feel of him against her body.

The moment the men walked past, Luke dropped his hand and moved slightly away, still keeping in step. Christina wanted to cry. Because of her and her stupid *secret*, she had lost the best thing that had ever happened to her. And the worst part, she wasn't sure what to do to get him back. Her grandmother often said that anything meant to be, would be. Christina wasn't so sure about that. From the moment she met Luke, she had felt that he was the one for her. That they were meant to be together. How could she have been so wrong? And what could she do to fix it?

"I'm right up here." She pointed to the next red brick building on her right. The old warehouse had been converted into lofts twenty years ago.

"I know."

She wondered what else he knew. Had he asked Zack about her?

She took out her key card and accepted her bag of food from him. The moment felt like the first time she had gone out with him, and he had taken her home. Like then, she didn't want to say goodbye.

"Would you like to come in?"

"No," he said without missing a beat, his gaze steady on her.

All righty then. She tried not to take offense, but she would be lying if she said that that one word hadn't cut deep.

He stood back, his hand in his pocket and his dark eyes boring into her.

"Okay, well thanks again for walking me home. I know I said this before, but I'm sorry for the way things ended. I feel awful. I never meant to mislead you or hurt you. Just don't leave yet. Give me a chance to explain because we need to talk about—"

1. He lifted his hand and shook his head, stopping her words. "The last time you said that we needed to talk, you walked out on me."

"Technically, you're the one who left me standing in the middle of your living room."

"Christina," he growled her name. "The only thing that I'm going to say about any of this is that I thought we were building something special, but that night—"

"We were." She reached for his hand. "We were building something special. You meant … you mean so much to me. You and I, we fit. I screwed up something very special."

He slipped his hand from her grasp. "I'm not interested in talking and I sure as hell don't want to rehash—"

"Fine." She cut him off, wanting to throw her bag at him. He was acting like a total jackass, and she would have told him so, but she looked into his eyes and her heart stuttered.

The pain she saw caught her off guard. It was then she realized just how much she had hurt him.

He broke eye contact and glanced up the street, as if knowing what she was thinking.

"Have a good night, Luke."

His gaze found hers again. "Yeah, you too. And," he sighed, struggling with his words. Instead of saying anything, he pinched the bridge of his nose and shut his eyes. Seconds passed, and Christina held her breath. She wasn't sure what she expected, but her stomach churned in anticipation. She needed him to forgive her and give them another chance. He finally looked at her. "Listen … it was good seeing you again."

Now she was the one who wanted to say more, but didn't. She nodded and unlocked the door, forcing her feet to take her inside, away from the man who tempted her to make a complete fool of herself by asking him for another chance.

CHAPTER FOUR

The next day, Christina rambled around her luxury loft near downtown Cincinnati. She stepped over boxes that still needed to be unpacked, thinking about the brief encounter with Luke. The chemistry sparking between them last night was as potent as ever, even if his mouth said otherwise. She not only felt the spark, she saw it in his eyes. A lot of good that did though. She had no idea how to make things right. She had no idea how to get him to listen to what she had to say. She had no idea how to gain his forgiveness for not being completely honest.

Her grandmother's words floated around in her head. *Anything meant to be will be.* This was one of those times she needed to have faith, and trust this situation would work itself out. In the meantime, she had to get ready for her visitors. Her sister Peyton and their cousins, Toni, Jada, and Martina were expected in fifteen minutes to help unpack.

Christina jumped at the sound of her door buzzer. Hurrying to the wall near the entrance, which held a monitor and an intercom, she saw her cousins standing in front of the camera. She grinned when Martina Jenkins, a.k.a. MJ stuck her tongue out at the camera. A carpenter by trade, that girl was the silliest of them all as well as the one person who

31

drove the entire family nuts most days, but loyal to a fault.

Christina swung the door open just as MJ started to knock. "Hey, you guys."

"All I want to know is what's up with that piece of crap you call an elevator?" MJ asked the moment she stepped across the threshold. "That thing is an accident waiting to happen." The dilapidated freight elevator was Christina's favorite part of the converted warehouse, giving the modern space a little rustic vibe. It serviced her unit only, which happened to be on the top floor.

"At least it had automatic doors and we didn't have to lift them." Toni Jenkins-Logan kissed Christina on the cheek and walked in. "What's up Cuz?"

"Not much, but couldn't you have left MJ wherever you found her?" Christina asked.

"Nope. She was driving."

"Hey, Sis." Peyton Jenkins stepped in with her hands full. She handed Christina a potted sunflower and carried the additional bags into the loft.

"Ahh, thanks, PJ!"

Before Christina could admire the plant in her hands, Jada "JJ" Jenkins-Anderson stepped into the doorway. Christina shook her head and grinned. Despite JJ's frustrated pout and her hands on her hips, she looked as stylish as usual in a white halter dress and matching four-inch sandals. Only she would show up at a box-unpacking-party looking like she just walked off of the cover of Vogue magazine.

"Remind me never to ride with them again," she said hugging Christina.

A month of not hanging out and seeing Jada was way too long. They had lived together for years, sharing tubs of ice cream on bad days, and whispering about their deep, dark secrets on other days. Christina couldn't be happier for her cousin and her new life with Zack, but she missed their girl talks.

"MJ must have been a NASCAR driver in another life,"

Jada said. "She drives like a dang maniac." Christina laughed, knowing that MJ broke every speed limit to get them there, which was why Christina never rode anywhere with her.

Christina closed the door and carried her new plant over to a rod-iron plant stand that stood near one of the floor to ceiling windows.

"I assume you know the plant is from mom. She said sunflowers are your favorite."

"They are."

Peyton frowned. "You two have to be the strangest women I know. Most people love roses or tulips, but no you guys have to be different. Oh, and she said that she'll stop by tomorrow. She has her aerial yoga class tonight or was it her nude yoga class?" She threw her arms out, letting them fall against the side of her thighs. "I don't know. I can't keep up with all of her different activities. I don't know how dad puts up with her."

Christina smiled and rearranged some of the plants. "Dad once told me that he fell in love with mom because of her style, uniqueness, and her inner freak. It turns him on the way she licks—"

"Stop! Yuck." Peyton covered her ears and shivered. "A visual suddenly popped into my head, and not one I want associated with my mother. I can't even believe he told you that."

Christina laughed at her sister's reaction. "Well, I was going to say a Popsicle. What were you thinking?"

"Oh. Um … never mind."

Their mother might not have been born until after the hippie movement, but she loved everything about that generation and still held on to some of the subculture. Peyton was her opposite - prim and proper to the bone. Christina on the other hand, knew she had inherited her mother's free-spirited attitude. For years, she had kept it concealed for fear of what people would say, but while dating Luke, a little of her real self had showed.

Toni stood in the middle of the living room. "This place is gorgeous. I love the exposed duct work, the floor to ceiling windows, and I can't believe I'm going to say this, but your vintage furniture looks perfect in here."

Christina ran her hand along the velvet, fuchsia sofa, a super find at her favorite consignment shop. Her design style, a combination of eclectic with a mixture of old and new styles, suited her personality perfect.

Her cousins, except for Jada, roamed around the 1700 square foot loft. It was thanks to Jada and Zack that CJ was living her dream of owning a loft. Zack had purchased the space years ago in order to have a place close to the stadium.

"I see you've painted," Jada said when Christina walked up to her and draped her arm over Jada's shoulders. "It looks good, but I'm surprised you left the living room white."

"I'm still debating the color I want in here. I'm thinking about pulling a color from one of the floral throw pillows. Maybe a bold gold tone. Or something in the green family."

"This place *is* nice." Peyton stood near the large, bare windows that overlooked downtown Cincinnati, her arms folded across her chest. The building sat on a slight hill, allowing for a spectacular view of the city. "I just want to know how you were able to afford something like this on your salary," her sister said over her shoulder.

Christina felt more than saw Jada look at her, probably wondering if she was going to come clean about her other life. Maybe she would one day, but today wasn't that day.

"Saving," Christina said without elaborating. "All right, I'm thinking that we should unpack a few of these boxes and then eat." She had moved in almost a week ago, but hadn't gotten around to unpacking much. When Toni had called to see if she was showing up for their weekly after work drink at their favorite bar and grill, Christina suggested they all meet at the loft.

"You must be crazy in your head if you think I'm going

to work before I eat. What's wrong with you?" MJ asked from the kitchen. "Okay, plates? Where are the plates?"

"In that box near the refrigerator marked, *plates*." Christina rolled her eyes. She already knew it was going to be a long night. "So what's for dinner?"

"Hamburgers and fries."

"MJ, what the heck? You know I'm a vegetarian."

"*Still*? I thought you would've given that up by now." Everyone but Christina laughed.

"And why would you think that?"

"Oh, come on CJ, like you don't know." Toni rinsed her hands in the kitchen sink and began pulling food out of the grease stained bags. "How many times have you started something and didn't finish?"

"More times than I can count," Peyton muttered, sitting on one of the barstools at the kitchen counter. "Like piano lessons, sculpting class, and ice skating to name a few."

"Don't forget guitar lessons," MJ said pulling out several hamburgers. The divine smell of bacon and onions made Christina's mouth water as she breathed in deep, tempted to fall victim to quitting yet another one of her goals.

"Oh, and my personal favorite – word-a-day," Jada said sarcastically and they all burst out laughing.

"Now that one, I'm glad she quit because I was about ready to strangle her with all of her big words." MJ stuck a fry in her mouth and grinned. "Who walks around using words like veneration in a simple sentence when she can use honoring?" They all pointed at Christina.

"You know what? Forget every single one of you." Christina pulled a leftover vegetable casserole from the refrigerator. "I can't help it if you're catachrestic and don't know what sesquipedalian or prehensile means. You're lucky I don't go all bellicose on you simpletons. Maybe one of these days when you flibbertigibbets get off my back and learn some new words, you won't look like the illiterates that you are."

They all stood opened mouth staring at her and then lost it. Pounding on the counter, Martina fell out laughing while Peyton and Toni held their stomachs cackling just as hard. Jada grinned trying to hold back but gave up and burst into a fit of giggles as well. Christina couldn't help but join in. She had given up on learning a word a day, but now realized how much she missed the reaction the words evoked when she used so many of them in one conversation.

The next forty-five minutes, they cracked jokes and talked. Christina's heart warmed as they laughed and swiped away happy tears, their banter livelier than usual. For the last three or four weeks, they hadn't been able to meet consistently. At work, she and MJ were on the same job, renovating a strip mall. Jada had left the company shortly after getting married and Toni, a master plumber, had cut her hours, only working part-time since giving birth to Craig Jr. five months earlier. She saw Peyton almost every day since her sister was the boss. Yet, Christina didn't realize how much she missed having all of them together until now. Sure they got on each other's nerves, but they were the best of friends and more importantly, family.

"Okay, where do you want me to start?" Toni asked, crumbling the burger wrapper and tossing the remains in the trash. "Craig and the baby will be here to pick me up in a couple of hours." Of course, after she mentioned the baby, she fielded questions about Craig Jr. and his latest accomplishments. They all stood around Toni's cell phone, cooing and gushing over photos and short videos of him rolling over from his back to his tummy and trying to scoot around.

Hearing Toni talk about Craig, and their little one, sent a bit of longing through Christina. Until recently, even at the age of twenty-nine, she hadn't thought much about marriage and having a family. Not until Luke.

Christina mentally shook herself. She wasn't going to let thoughts of him invade her mind tonight. Not like the last two days. Awake or asleep, dreaming about Luke left her frustrated and horny. So many times, she had wondered what they would say or do if they ran into each other again. Somehow Christina had imagined their first run-in going differently. Very differently. They had only dated for a few months, but during that time, she found a connection and freedom she hadn't known existed. Spending time with him made her want to live life on purpose and be who she really was, not what others expected her to be.

"Earth calling CJ. Come in CJ." Jada waved her hand in front of Christina's face. "Where'd you go? Toni wants to know where to start."

"Oh." Christina glanced around at her cousins who were looking at her strangely. "How about in the kitchen?" Christina loved the kitchen. With the high-end stainless steel appliances, dark granite countertops, and maple custom-made cabinets, everything was top of the line.

"Sounds good," Toni said.

"I'll help in here too since there are tons of boxes marked kitchen, and I remember how you had the cabinets organized at the other house," Jada said.

"Why is this door locked?" MJ asked from across the room and down a short hallway that could still be seen from the kitchen. She stood at the door to the second bedroom.

"Oh, I need to get the key from Zack," Christina lied. She knew someone would ask about that room and had already planned her response.

"Why the heck did he need a locked room? Did he have some sex apparatus or kinky toys in here?" MJ lifted a perfectly arched eyebrow, directing her question at Jada.

"Yep," Jada said, the lie rolling off her tongue. She knew Zack used the space as a guest room and she was the only person who knew what Christina had on the other side of the door.

Christina would have to thank her cousin later.

She walked into her bedroom and stopped short when her

sister held a painting, her bulging eyes revealing her shock.

"What is this?" Peyton turned the canvas around to Christina.

"Art."

"Don't get smart. You know what I mean. What's gotten into you? Not even mom has naked people hanging on the walls." The painting in question was a Sasha Knight original. One of the artist's most provocative pieces and Christina's favorite. "I can't believe you bought something like this."

"It's a work of art." Christina took the painting, and leaned it against one of the bedroom walls then stepped back to peruse it. Tastefully done, the silhouette of a couple making love up against a wall with a streak of moonlight, from the window next to them, casting a glow over their sweat slicked bodies. Sexy without being vulgar. The contours of their joined bodies angled just right had no private parts exposed except for one of the man's firm butt cheeks. The painting reminded her of her affair with Luke and the passion they once shared.

"Surely you're not planning to have some naked couple hanging on your walls." Her sister's incredulous tone was in line with her rigid, walk-a-straight-line attitude. "What will people think?"

Christina turned to her sister. "I don't care what people think. They don't have to come over here if they have a problem with my art collection." For the past few years, her collection had grown to over twenty pieces. She barely had enough wall space to hang half of the pieces.

"So you don't have a problem with Gramma or Grampa seeing that?" Peyton pointed to the picture.

Christina narrowed her eyes at her sister and then returned her gaze to the piece of art. Okay maybe she did have a problem with *them* seeing a nude painting hanging on her wall, but they rarely stopped by for a visit.

"You know what? I blame that guy, Luke, for this reckless attitude of yours. Maybe it's good you two broke up. He might have been a big-time New York lawyer, but he was a bad influence on you. The piercings," she said referring to the tiny diamond stud in Christina's nose, "now paintings of naked people. Yeah, he was definitely a bad influence."

"No, he wasn't!" Christina said. "You can talk about me all you want, but leave him out of this. That man was the best thing that ever happened to me."

"So what's next tattoos?" Peyton's tone was judgmental, but Christina had stopped caring that her sister didn't approve of the way she lived her life. Especially lately.

"Maybe."

"Are you kidding me?" She shook her head and folded her arms across her chest. "You know what, whatever. I'm just glad you came to your senses and broke up with Luke. Maybe now you'll get back to normal instead of walking around looking like … like Lisa Bonet with the wild hair, Bohemian clothes and—"

"Dang Peyton, can't you give it a rest?" Jada asked from the doorway.

"You need to stay out of this, Jada," Peyton said.

"No, you're the one who needs to stay out of it. You know how much CJ cared for Luke, and you're in here talking bad about him? What's that all about? Maybe if you found your own man, you could stay out of everyone else's love life."

Christina knew Jada regretted the words the moment they left her mouth. Peyton, divorced for several years, hadn't dated since then. Her whole life was Jenkins & Sons Construction. They all wanted her to get back out there and find love, but her failed marriage or any reference to a social life, was a sore spot with her.

"PJ, I'm sorry. I shouldn't have said that," Jada apologized.

"No, you're right. What CJ does or who she does it with is none of my business." Peyton stormed passed Jada.

"That went well …or not." Christina dropped down on the corner of the bed and shook her head. Just once, it would be nice for them to get together without someone getting mad or getting their feelings hurt. Normally it was Martina getting on someone's nerve, but lately, Peyton seemed to be taking her unhappiness out on everyone.

"Me and my big mouth. I should've minded my own business and let you handle your sister." Jada walked farther into the room and sat next to Christina. "I just can't stand to hear her giving you a hard time about Luke, especially since I know he's a good guy."

Yeah, he was a good guy, Christina thought. Until she let him walk out of her life. If she could just get a do over, she would do things differently.

"Don't worry about it. I'm not sure what her problem is these days."

"I know." Jada crossed her leg and leaned back on her elbows. "Toni told me that she's been a pain at work too. What she needs is a warm body to curl up with and maybe expend some of that pent up anger doing the horizontal tango."

Christina threw back her head and laughed. "Oh, so you get some on the regular now and think that's the answer to all problems?"

"Hey, I'm just sayin'." They giggled and slapped high five.

It had been awhile since Christina had done anything horizontal, but she had to admit. A couple of rounds of some good lovin' always made everything feel right in the world.

"I'm glad you're back," she said to Jada. "See what you've been missing around here. You go off and get married and miss out on all the fun."

After marrying Zack, Jada had quit her job as a sheet metal worker. No one was really surprised. Jada was allergic to manual labor.

Christina glanced over her shoulder at Jada and smiled.

"You look good … happy. Marriage is agreeing with you."

Jada sat forward and held her small hand out, the cluster of diamonds on her ring finger sparkling. "Marriage is unbelievable." She lowered her hand. "You know I get on Zack's nerve, but that man has to be the sweetest person that ever walked the face of the earth. He puts up with my nonsense, but he's like a boulder when he doesn't want to do something or doesn't approve of something. Even my pouts can't move him. And I can pout." Jada pursed her lips and folded her arms. Her lips curled into a pout, and they both laughed. Christina knew all too well how Jada used to get what she wanted from whomever she wanted. Including Zack.

The family had been shocked to find out the couple had eloped to Las Vegas, especially since Jada had always talked about having a wedding fit for a princess. When Christina had asked why she forewent a wedding, Jada told her that she didn't need all the hoopla that went with a large wedding when she had the man of her dreams. Her once self-centered cousin was a different person, proving that falling in love could change anyone. Now, she was married, volunteering at non-profit organizations and taking college classes in fashion.

"So have you talked to him since he's been in Cincinnati?" Jada asked, cutting into Christina's thoughts.

Christina knew the *him* was Luke. Jada was the only one of her cousins who knew Luke fairly well since he and Zack were good friends. But since her cousin had been traveling over the last few months, they hadn't had a chance to discuss the break up in detail.

"I saw him."

"What? And you didn't tell me?"

"Nothing to tell. I saw him the other night when I was walking home." She filled her cousin in on the encounter and included how he turned her down when she invited him into her place. "I don't know what I expected. That last night in

New York, he was pretty mad."

"I don't blame him."

"What? How can you say that?" Christina knew she could have and should have handled things differently with Luke, but she couldn't believe Jada condoned his behavior.

"CJ get serious. *You* had suddenly decided to stay in New York instead of coming back to Cincinnati with him. That probably had him imagining the worse. The poor guy probably didn't know what to think."

"He should have known me well enough to know that I had a good reason. It had nothing to do with being involved with another man."

"How would he know that? You guys were still getting to know each other, and it was a long distance relationship. I'm sure he had no idea that there were secrets between you two. You could have handled that situation differently. You *should* have handled it differently especially if he meant anything to you."

"Do you still care for him?"

"There hasn't been a day that's gone by that I haven't thought about him. I know you never believed in everyone having a soul mate, but I honestly believe that he's mine."

"I don't know if I necessarily believe that everyone has a soul-mate, but being married to Zack has made me consider the possibility. Falling in love with him was like finding the missing puzzle piece to my life. We fit. I'm a better person because of my hubby."

"You can say that again," Christina mumbled and then burst out laughing when Jada elbowed her in the arm almost knocking her off the bed. "I'm just sayin', you were a mess before he came along. Selfish, superficial, and I could go on."

"Yeah, well don't. We're not talking about the old me. We're talking about you. So answer me this, if you really cared about Luke, why didn't you just tell him months ago what was going on with you?"

Christina had asked herself that question a thousand times. Her other life had been a secret for so long, the thought of sharing it with anyone other than Jada seemed impossible.

"I'm not sure. I guess I just don't want any negative vibes circling me. When people don't understand something, they tend to shoot you down."

"I know I promised to keep this secret, but honestly, I don't see what the big deal is. So you have another life. So what? I kinda get why you haven't told the family, but why not Luke? Is it that you don't trust him?"

"At the time I was still getting to know him." The more she thought about it, the more she realized that she was making everything harder than it needed to be. "In hindsight I wish I would have just told him."

"He's a lawyer. Couldn't you have just given him a dollar and hired him? I think at that point, everything would have fallen under some client confidentiality thing."

Christina laughed. Leave it to Jada to come up with something like that. "I'll have to keep that in mind if ever he gives me a chance to make things right between us."

"So are you going to tell the family soon? You don't want them to hear from someone else."

"Yeah, I know. I guess I'm just afraid they'll judge me."

"They might, but you're a grown ass woman. Who cares what people think?"

"Honestly? I do." She had told her sister that she didn't care what others thought, but deep in her heart, she did care. "I don't want Grampa to be disappointed in me."

"Oh please. If he can get over Toni being arrested or get over all the nonsense that I've been a part of, he can deal with your stuff."

"Yeah … maybe."

CHAPTER FIVE

Sitting in his office, Luke took out his cell phone and pulled up a picture he had taken of Christina during her last visit to New York. Despite being angry at her, he couldn't bring himself to delete the photo. After seeing her three days ago, he couldn't stop thinking about her. Just when he thought he had moved on – bam. She shot back into his life like a meteor plummeting to earth, leaving a trail of her lust-inducing scent.

He tapped his cell phone screen, increasing the size of the photo and stared into eyes that had enraptured him from day one. And that smile. God he had missed her smile. When they were dating, the highlight of his evening after a tough day in court was seeing Christina. Either he would go home to her when she visited or they would Skype and talk well into the night.

Frustration pumped through his veins as he stifled a groan. There had to be a way to get her out of his system. He wanted a simple life, and whatever she was hiding, was probably anything but simple.

He glanced up when he heard a soft knock at his opened office door.

"Are you ready for me?" Robin Drake, his paralegal asked. The suggestiveness of her words matched the seductive smile on her lips.

Luke gave her a once over wondering how she managed to get away with dressing like she was going partying with her girlfriends – thin blouse, short skirt, stilettos and all.

He waved her in. "Sure, we can meet now." He shoved his cell phone back into his pocket. Not sure what he was going to do about Christina, he knew if he ever wanted to get some sleep again, he had to do something. Thinking about her all day and dreaming about her at night was starting to take its toll.

Robin caught his attention when she made a production of pulling the guest chair in front of his desk back a few inches. She lowered her fit body and crossed her long legs.

"Where would you like to start?"

Luke ignored the sultriness of her voice and pulled a pile of files in front of him. "Jason Lake. I'll need to talk to Gary regarding that case." Days after Luke had started with the firm, Gary had given him several cases that he'd been overseeing, claiming that most of them just needed some follow-up. Not only did they need follow-up, there were two that Gary hadn't even started. The attorney had barely interviewed the clients. "There's not enough evidence to prove that Deluxe Construction did anything wrong. Unless Gary hasn't given me everything. So let's hold off on that one."

Luke pulled out the third file in his pile and handed it to Robin. "I'm not working with Mr. Hardy. There's no way I can work with that man for the next two years with his attitude. And it will take at least that long and an infinite stream of funds to prove his claim. After our conversation last week, he won't be surprised that I turned down the case."

There was a time when Luke would take almost every case that came across his desk, but those days were long gone.

For the next twenty minutes, they went over a few more cases. When deciding to leave criminal law, he wasn't sure what or where he'd practice. His biggest concern was that any other type of law wouldn't hold his interest. Though some days he missed the intensity that came with taking on murder cases, this slower pace wasn't all bad.

"Is there anything else I can do for you?"

Luke slowly lifted his head from the file in front of him, his eyebrow cocked at the sensual tone of his paralegal's question. At the rate she was going, they were definitely going to have to have *the* talk. The talk where he told her he wasn't interested in anything outside of a working relationship. Robin, a pretty red head with flawless skin and too tight clothes had been making suggestive comments to him since the day he started. It wasn't so much the comments or the questions, but more so the way she phrased them. Every question she asked sounded like a proposition and spoken with a seductive tone. A tone that would make any red-blooded man stand at attention. But Luke had had just about enough.

"I'll also need everything you can find on the owners of the Pearson Corporation. I mean everything. Bank information, cell phone records. If they're married, children - everything."

"No problem. Anything for you." She scribbled on her notepad.

"Oh and can you finish your report on the Hudson case by Friday? I want to make sure we're ready to present the information to the client next week."

His gaze fell to her legs. How many times had she crossed and recrossed her legs causing her skirt to rise and show more leg than should be allowed in a professional environment? He would admit, she was a beautiful woman, but he wasn't interested. She might have garnered his attention, but there was only one woman who ever made him want to throw caution to the wind and try something he had never tried – being in a committed relationship.

He set his pen down and sat back in the seat. Propping his elbow on the arm of his office chair, he rubbed his forehead. Thinking of Christina was driving him nuts. Robin offered a momentary distraction, but her antics just made him long for Christina that much more. Problem was, any chance they might have had at reconciling had been shot to hell thanks to him. He could have handled their run-in better. Actually, any other behavior from him would have been better than making her think that he didn't still care. Heck, he more than cared and that's what scared the hell out of him.

His phone vibrated and chirped, signaling a text message. Before he could pull the device from his pocket, Robin cleared her throat. He knew he was tired, but rarely did he zone out to the point of forgetting she was sitting in front of him.

She stood and leaned over the front of his desk, giving him a clear view of her lacy pink bra. His gaze lingered there for a hot second before lifting his eyes to meet hers.

"It's almost lunch time. Would you like to eat out?"

Luke had spent most of his career reading body language, as well as in between the lines. Though she asked the question innocently enough, the look in her green eyes and the seductive smile on her ruby red lips, said otherwise.

"If you value your job Ms. Drake, I suggest you start wearing attire that's befitting of a professional environment." The smile slipped from her lips, and she stood straighter, adjusting her low-cut blouse. "Also, I'm not sure how things work with the other attorneys you support, but whatever you're offering, I'm not interested."

"I … I don't know what you mean." She fidgeted with the pen in her hand.

Luke stood and smoothed down his Versace tie. "I think you do." Not wanting his frankness to come back and bite him in the ass, he added, "You're an excellent paralegal, and

I like working with you professionally. I wouldn't want there to be any misunderstanding that would hurt our working relationship."

She nodded and attempted a smile that didn't reach her eyes. "I wouldn't want that either. I'll take care of these items," she mumbled and lifted the files from his desk. She started to say more but seemed to think better of it and left his office.

After she had gone, Luke sighed and dropped back down into his seat. Every day he'd been questioning his decision to relocate. Between Robin, Gary, and the office as a whole, some days he wondered if he had made the right decision.

His cell phone vibrated again, reminding him that he hadn't checked the first message he had received before addressing Robin.

Digging the phone from the interior pocket of his suit jacket, he tapped the screen. His heart leaped around in his chest just as it did whenever he nailed a closing argument in court.

Christina.

Staring down at his cell, he frowned trying to figure out what he was looking at on the screen. "What the ..." An image of what appeared to be a picture of a lung covered the screen, followed by a similar image. There was no doubt that these were diseased lungs, considering the dark discoloration of the organ.

His phone vibrated again, but this time with a message.

Keep smoking & this is what ur lungs r going 2 look like. As u told me, I care about ... your safety.

Well, damn.

He sat staring at the photos and then her message. A smile crept across his lips, and he chuckled. *Talk about making a point.* She had often voiced her dislike of his habit, but this was the first time she'd added images to express her point.

A warm sensation flowed through his body. Apparently,

they'd been thinking about each other.

He laid his cell on top of a file folder without responding to the message, his fingers tapping on the desk. He was down to one cigarette a day, usually having one right after work. Knowing he needed to give them up and doing it was one of the hardest things he'd ever tried accomplishing, but right now, he needed to figure out what to do about Christina. On second thought, there was nothing to figure out. He wanted to see her. It was time he stopped pretending he didn't. But first he owed her an apology for the way he had walked away the other day. When what he wanted to do was pull her into his arms and cover her mouth with his. Kissing her had once been his favorite pastime. Hell, anything with her was his favorite pastime.

He picked up his cell phone and tapped against the screen.

Thanks. I appreciate your concern. Need something to distract me from the smokes though.

Minutes ticked by and just as he started to wonder if she would respond, a text came through.

Is that right?

He grinned, enjoying their banter. **That's correct. Any ideas?**

Yeah, one.

Okay, I'll bite. **And what's that?**

Yoga.

Luke threw his head back and laughed. She knew good and damn well yoga wasn't an option. There's been only one thing that distracted him from wanting a smoke. Okay, maybe two things, but they both involved one person.

Christina "CJ" Jenkins.

Instead of texting her, he dialed her number.

"Hello." She answered on the first ring.

"Hey." Luke had never had a problem talking to women or going after what he wanted. Until now. Until Christina. Everything about this woman turned him on and threw him off his game. He wanted her, but the one thing he couldn't tolerate – being lied to. He had always been slow to trust. To know she had lied to him on more than one occasion, still didn't sit well with him. However, she had somehow bulldozed her way into his heart and now held a certain amount of power that no other woman had ever come close to possessing. And this scared him to death.

"Luke?"

"Yeah, I'm here. I was just ..." His words were lodged in his throat, surprising the hell out of him. He had spent his adult life, arguing some of the most grueling cases, yet at that moment, words escaped him. Rubbing the back of his neck, he knew what he needed to do, but apologizing never came easy for him. Heck, he couldn't remember the last time he had expressed regret to anyone for anything, but he did what he should have done days ago. "Look, I'm sorry about the other day. I was a total ass."

"Yeah ... you were." She chuckled, and Luke felt a smile form on his lips. "But, I think you were entitled. I'm the one who caused this strain between us." She might have been the one who started them in the wrong direction, but he knew shutting the door on their relationship was all him.

"It takes two and I know I'm not the most understanding or the easiest person to talk to, but ..." he shrugged as if she could see him, "I am who I am. You were right the other night when you said we needed to talk. Can we hook up tonight or tomorrow?"

"I'd like that. How about tonight? Do you want to stop by my place?"

Luke was barely able to rein in his libido after seeing her the other night. If he went to her place, he had no doubt where things would end up. Christina had been the first woman he'd ever met whose sexual appetite was as intense as his and intimacy had never been a problem between them. He wanted her. He wanted her so bad his body ached just thinking about the last time they were together in that way.

"I'm not sure meeting at your place is a good idea."

After a long pause, she said, "Actually, it'll be better if we talked in private and there's something I need to show you ... here, at my place. Maybe we can start here and then if you want, we can leave and go somewhere else." When Luke didn't respond, she continued. "Luke, nothing will happen, that you don't want to happen."

Yeah, that's what he was afraid of. He wanted *it* to happen, and he was sure *it* would happen whether they intended on *it* happening or not.

"How about we go out to eat or maybe have a drink and then see what happens afterward." Being out in public would give them a chance to get reacquainted and force him to keep his hands and lips off of her.

An hour later, Luke sat across from Christina trying not to stare at her. Not only did she look incredibly sexy, she hadn't given him a hard time about changing his mind and suddenly wanting to talk. Instead, she readily agreed to meet him and was sitting across from him as if he hadn't slighted her days ago.

His gaze raked over her while she talked on her cell phone, giving her sister, Peyton, information regarding a job. Dressier than usual, tonight she wore a low-cut, white sleeveless blouse showing off well-toned arms and flat abs. His shaft had leaped to attention when she had walked into the bar looking sexier than he had ever seen her. She was already the total package but swathed in a seductive outfit, she was like a Christmas present begging to be unwrapped. The fitted black skirt that molded over her shapely hips and stopped just above her knees, with a wide black belt that emphasized her narrow waist, had him glancing away to keep from salivating.

Luke wondered if what he felt the other night upon seeing Christina had been a fluke. The way his mouth had gone dry and how his body had come alive when his hand had made contact with the small of her back. The electric charge that shot up his arm that night was almost his undoing. And then there was the quiver that had flitted around in his gut, that hadn't let up until she was safely behind her closed door. She had stirred a longing within him that he struggled to contain and tonight was no different.

He lifted the glass of Scotch to his lips hoping the smoothness of the liquid would tap down his growing need to hold her, to see if her body still responded to his touch. Who knew one woman could shake him up like this? Never one for dating exclusively, Christina had been his first real relationship. Luke worked so much that he hadn't realized his life was missing anything – not until Christina had come along and shook up his world. He quickly remembered why he didn't do relationships. When they parted ways, it was as if he had lost a part of himself. He never wanted to experience that type of pain again. He had already lost his parents, the people who had meant the world to him. No way would he allow his heart to be ripped out of his chest again. Yet … here he was thinking about giving this relationship crap another shot.

"Sorry about that." Christina stuffed her cell phone back inside her large Coach bag. "PJ had been in meetings all afternoon and I needed to update her on certain aspects of the job I've been on."

"No problem. I'm glad you were able to meet me." Their gazes collided, and the air was knocked out of him. Tonight she reminded him of the first time he had met her at Zack's birthday party. Like then, he felt helpless in fighting his attraction to her. "I owe you an apology for the way I treated you the other night."

"You already apologized for that and actually, you don't owe me anything."

"I wasn't in the right frame of mind to hear anything you had to say. First of all, I was in shock from running into you, but also still a little pissed by the way we parted."

"And that was my fault. I could have handled that night

in New York better than I had." She stared down at her hands that were wrapped around her drink. She had ordered a cosmopolitan, which was interesting since she was usually a wine drinker. Luke watched as her fingers traced the condensation on the outside of the glass, remembering her soft touch against his body.

He shifted in his seat, catching himself before he allowed his mind to travel back to a time when they couldn't keep their hands off of each other.

"I never meant to hurt you," she mumbled, not meeting his eyes.

The attorney in Luke wanted to bombard her with question after question. He wanted, no he needed to talk about that night, but he wasn't sure if he was ready to dig deeper, ready to find out what she was hiding. It had to be her decision to share why she walked away from what they had. He wouldn't push. Instead, he had to figure out whether or not she was worth fighting for. And if he had to decide at that moment, his answer would be a hell yeah.

He moved his chair closer to Christina's and looped his arm over her shoulders, his hand playing in her long tresses. Each time she moved, her hair swayed, and the scent of wildflowers tickled his nose. How many nights had he pulled her close to get a better whiff of her hair?

"Where do we go from here?" he asked.

Christina placed her hand on his thigh. The scorching heat from her touch sent a lightning bolt of need charging through his body.

"I've missed you so much."

The desire in her eyes matched what he felt. Instead of responding, he placed a finger under her chin and pulled her closer. He did what he wanted to do the other night. His mouth touched hers first tentatively, but soon the softness of her lips had him begging for more, and he took what he wanted.

He missed her too. He missed this - their connection,

their ability to know what the other needed, and a willingness to supply those needs. Heat radiated through his body and the caress of her lips against his mouth, sent spirals of ecstasy shooting straight to his shaft. Her passionate moans, God he loved the sexy sounds she made, urging him on.

Christina put her hands on each side of his face, and she pulled back slightly, resting her forehead against his. "Why don't we get out of here?"

*

Christina was so horny she was about to lose her damn mind. Three months, three weeks and one day. That's how long it had been since she'd been with Luke. Since she'd been with anyone. It didn't help that he had just kissed her the same way he used to, thoroughly and completely. Making the lustful ache in her core throb that much more. She was wound so tight that if he put his hands or mouth on her at any point in the next few minutes, she couldn't be sure that she wouldn't jump into his arms and beg him to make love to her.

Even now, standing at the entrance to her building with him, her body pulsed with awareness. He didn't even have to touch her. The heat from his presence did enough to send desire pumping through her veins.

She unlocked the door. It had only taken them fifteen minutes to get to her loft, and she played Luke's words around in her mind.

Where do we go from here?

She so wanted to make things right between them. Not just because the kiss they shared at the bar made her toes curl, and she never wanted the intense lip-lock to end, but because she missed him something terrible. She missed what they once had. Whether they could pick up where they left off remained to be seen.

Christina led him to the elevator and punched in her code. Zack had paid a small fortune to have the elevator set up to only service the sixth floor.

The doors finally slid open, and Christina stepped in. Luke stood in the hall looking as if he had no intention of taking the elevator, his arms folded across his chest.

"You do know that this thing is a death trap don't you? I can't begin to tell you how many times Zack and I have been stuck on this piece of shit."

Christina grinned. "Actually, he did tell me a few stories."

"And you're still using it?" He didn't look too pleased, but it made Christina feel good to know that he cared about her. Either that or he was just afraid to get on.

"Zack had it serviced before he sold me the loft. Besides, it has a telephone." She pointed to the red phone near the up and down button. "He set up a direct link to 911."

"That doesn't make me feel any better," Luke mumbled. Seeing that she wasn't getting off, he stepped on. "I still don't think it's safe, especially when you're by yourself."

The doors closed, and Luke pressed the up button. The elevator started its usual slow climb but jerked a little. Something it did each time Christina rode up to her loft. Luke glanced down at her and reached for her hand, pulling her closer to him. It took everything she had not to burst out laughing at the frown on his face.

She lifted their joined hands, unable to keep the grin off her face. "Are you scared?"

"Of course not. I'm holding your hand to make sure you're not afraid." His mouth twitched, fighting the smile that she knew lingered in the not so far distance.

Christina leaned against the wall of the elevator and almost sighed when Luke's thumb caressed the back of her hand. Considering how rigid he was standing, she didn't think he realized that his touch was driving her nuts, sending a sweet tingle through her body. Stoking the flame that he had already started with the kiss he planted on her back at the bar. If he was holding her hand, maybe that was a good sign the relationship could be repaired. She knew he didn't forgive easily, but maybe he had already forgiven her for the way things ended months ago. She could only hope.

When the elevator finally came to a stop, and the doors opened, they stepped off and stood in the quiet hall. The sixth floor had once had two small units, but Zack had purchased both of them, combining them into one large space. The last time her cousin MJ had been there, she had commented that Zack should have had the elevator doors open right into the unit. Christina was glad he hadn't. She liked the idea of having the hallway and a separate door to her loft. Any other way would have felt weird.

"Come on in," she said to Luke after unlocking the door and walking in. "Make yourself at home."

Luke strolled over to the floor to ceiling windows, something everyone did when they first walked in. The sheer curtains framing the windows of the main living space stayed open most of the time, no one could see directly into the loft.

Christina set her handbag down and went into the kitchen. "Can I get you something to eat or drink?" They'd ordered an appetizer earlier and had a drink while at the bar, but she hadn't had dinner and she assumed he hadn't either.

He turned to her. The seriousness radiating in his eyes, let her know this conversation wasn't going to be easy. She diverted her gaze and let it trek down the length of his body. He had left his suit jacket in the car, and the sleeves of his white collared striped shirt had been rolled up to the center of his forearms. Now he was loosening his tie.

"Water would be good, thanks. I like what you've done with the place. It looks like you." He walked over and studied an abstract piece of art from her collection hanging on the living room wall. It blended an array of colors also represented in the furniture as well as the accessories. "This place suits you. It's warm," he moved closer, his voice seductively deep, "and understated, sexy."

Christina swallowed hard. If he moved any closer, she was going to rip off his clothes and take matters into her own hands. Thankfully, he stopped at the edge of the breakfast bar. She fidgeted as his penetrating gaze bore into her, stoking a gently growing fire within her. Clearly he still affected her like no other man ever had.

She slid his bottle of water closer to him, making sure not to touch his hand. If she kept her distance, she could get her thundering heart to settle down and not beat right out of her chest.

"Thanks." He took a hefty swig of the water. Maybe she wasn't the only one experiencing a certain type of heat that had nothing to do with the temperature inside the loft.

"So are you ready to tell me what happened back in New York?"

No, is what she wanted to say, but she knew it was now or never.

"I can show you better than I can tell you. Follow me." She had her keys out and was standing near the locked bedroom door when she realized he hadn't moved from his spot near the kitchen counter. They stood staring at each other and though she wasn't sure what he was thinking, she could guess. At this point, he didn't know what to expect from her. "I promise I won't hurt you," she cracked and pushed the door open, disappearing inside.

CHAPTER SIX

Damn.

The last thing Luke needed to do was follow Christina Jenkins into a bedroom. Any bedroom. The woman was like his kryptonite. It was already taking everything he had not to pull her in for another kiss. There was no way he would be able to keep his hands off of her in a bedroom. After the kiss at the bar, he was tempted to pull her into a nearby bathroom to finish what they had started. When she suggested they leave the bar, he followed behind her on autopilot. He would have followed her to the ends of the earth to indulge in whatever she offered.

When Christina stepped into the bedroom, he took a deep breath and followed. She had said earlier that nothing would happen that he didn't want to happen. Surely she knew him well enough to know what he wanted to happen.

He stopped short at the open door, and his mouth went dry. This was not what he expected. Luke didn't know how long he stood at the door gawking at what lay beyond the threshold.

"I swear to you I never lied about anything except for when it concerned my work or the art shows."

Luke roamed around the intimate space. Some of Christina's half-truths, like why she insisted they visit so many galleries each time she visited New York came to mind. He was sure that if he thought hard enough, other moments would trigger a memory of when she might have lied to him.

Shocked by what he was seeing, and unsure at the same time, Luke stepped farther into the room. Paintings of all shapes and sizes, landscapes, abstract and even nudes littered every available space. Some were even sitting on top of drop cloths covering the floor and propped against the wall. But there was one piece that drew him like a magnet to metal. Breathtakingly striking, a masterpiece sat on an easel more magnificent than any work of art he had seen at any gallery.

"If you haven't guessed it yet, I'm Sasha Knight."

Well, I'll be damned.

So many instances of their times together made sense now. Luke didn't know whether to be pissed by the fact that she had lied to him on more than one occasion or to bow down to her extraordinary talent. She had a gift, a serious gift if she had created everything in the room.

He continued to peruse the artwork.

"How long have you been painting?" He glanced over his shoulder, surprised to see her standing near the door, her bottom lip between her teeth, insecurity shining in her eyes. He had no idea what that expression was all about, but he planned to find out before he left there tonight. "I guess a better question would be, when did you start working with canvas?"

She had once told him that she started her painter apprenticeship months after graduating from high school. But this, his gaze swept over the paintings again, this went way beyond anything an apprenticeship could offer.

"I've always been fascinated with art, either drawing or paintings. I didn't start getting serious about my work until about five years ago." She had taken a few steps toward him, but still kept her distance.

Luke had an overwhelming desire to reach for her hand and pull her closer, but he resisted. The fact remained she had lied to him. But, why?

"When I first started, I did one or two projects a year for fun. I had entered an art contest just for the heck of it, and this woman called and said she was an agent. She told me she had an offer I couldn't refuse. One thing led to another, and two years ago I had my first show in Chicago." She touched the edge of a canvas that was leaning against a paint-splattered chair. "Before I knew it, I had completed four shows with my fifth one only a month away."

"That seems like a lot in such a short amount of time," Luke said absently and turned back to her work, one piece in particular pulling at his attention. A nude. Though parts of the faces were shown, he couldn't make out the specifics of their facial features. Christina had used black, white, gray and beige paint to cast a slight shadow over some of the couple's contours, but revealed enough of their bodies for an observer to clearly make out what was going on. The longer Luke stared at the painting, the more he recognized the scene. New York. The blues of the bathroom tile behind the couple and the rectangular rainfall showerhead were identical to the doublewide shower in his Fifth Avenue apartment in Manhattan.

Luke rubbed a hand over his chest as if the simple move would slow his pounding heart. The thought that Christina had replicated one of the most provocative lovemaking sessions he had ever experienced sent heat soaring through his body.

His eyes took in more details. Water cascaded over the couple's naked bodies from the overhead shower as the man held one of the woman's shapely legs around his waist. The profile of the guy's head was visible. Luke could make out the intensity on the man's face as he made love to the woman.

The painting had captured just enough to take him back to that morning as if it were yesterday. He could still hear the same heart-pounding music pumping through the bathroom speakers, spurring him on as he slid in and out of Christina's sweet heat. Their moans intermingled with every thrust as he went deeper, harder, rocking her body as if his life depended on bringing her to climax over and over again. He remembered not being able to get enough of her.

"Is this one for sale?" he asked, his voice raspy with desire. The passion and the intensity between the couple leaped off the canvas. The visual combined with Luke's memory of that morning he and Christina had shared made his body throb with a need that threatened his sanity.

That day would forever be engrained in his mind. Not because of the intense lovemaking in the shower. No. It had everything to do with the night before when he realized he had fallen in love with Christina. Instead of voicing his feelings for her right then, the next morning in the shower he had attempted to show her just what he felt, sharing all the emotions that were sieving through his veins. The memory had his body thrumming with desire, willing and ready to pay whatever she wanted for the painting.

Luke took a deep breath and released it slowly, trying like hell to hold it together. Once he felt his heart rate and that twinge of irritation for the hell he had experienced over the last few months subside, he turned to her.

"It's not for sale," she said before he could open his mouth again.

Their eyes met. Clearly, the painting had the same effect on her. But no way could it mean more to her than it meant to him. Little did she know, but the picture depicted a defining moment in his life. The only time he had ever admitted to himself that he was in love with a woman. In love with Christina.

As if knowing he was about to make her an offer of an obscene amount of money for the painting, she shook her head no, never taking her eyes from his.

First to break eye contact, he studied the painting again. How she managed to capture that moment – that intense, earth-shattering moment, so perfectly blew his mind. No one but them would ever be able to tell who the models were and that made him realize something else. She had done the piece by memory.

Absolutely breathtaking.

Finally pulling himself away, he stepped to another nude painting of a man, leaning against a fireplace mantle, a drink in his hand. Tastefully done, she revealed just enough of his body but left plenty for the imagination. And next to that painting, a naked woman holding a red scarf that draped loosely across her breasts, and slid between her opened thighs. The material covered the most intimate parts of the woman's body, but still left enough of her exposed to keep the observer wondering what lay beneath.

"So why nudes?"

"Why not?" Christina's words loaded with attitude shot across the room faster than the speed of light.

Luke lifted his hands in mock surrender. "Hey, I'm not complaining. I'm even thinking about commissioning you to paint something for my place. I just wonder why the change. Your earlier work was landscapes and abstract. Then all of a sudden, you're doing a show of all nudes." Again, his mind took him back to that last night in New York. It was no wonder she had wanted to stay longer. She, Sasha Knight, had been the featured artist.

Sasha Knight. She's Sasha Knight. He couldn't wrap his brain around this new information.

"The human body fascinates me." Christina stepped over to another nude hanging on the wall. A couple staring lovingly into each other's eyes. In the painting, the woman's hand rested against the man's jaw and one of the man's hands on her hip. "Body parts, skin tones, and even one's imperfections. All of it. Fascinating."

Luke stared at the painting, noticing the slight love handles on the male figure. The dark discoloration around the woman's elbow and her slightly sagging breast were real. When he first looked at the painting, he zoned in on the pose and the way the couple touched each other. The tenderness of the scene so evident, he hadn't noticed any imperfections.

A lover of art, Luke was familiar with Sasha Knight's work and had even purchased one of her abstract pieces a year ago. Who knew he'd be sharing this moment with the talented artist?

He shook his head, rubbing his hand over the top of his hair and down to the back of his neck. Hell, he had shared a whole lot more than a moment with her. And all this time she never said a word. Never let on that she was Sasha Knight.

That twinge of annoyance from earlier slowly turned into anger. How could she not tell him? He felt like a damn fool. All this time and he never knew. He should've been able to figure it out himself. The signs were there. The evasive responses to his questions regarding some of her travels; her desire to visit practically every art gallery in New York, and her obsession with Sasha Knight. He should have known.

Luke glanced at Christina. "Our last night in New York, at the art gallery, you asked me what type of person I thought Sasha Knight was. Do you remember what I said?" Christina gave a slight nod. Luke turned back to the painting in front of him. "Like then, I think her talents shine through in the landscapes and abstract work, but there's something about the nudes that reveal a different side of her. She's someone who pays attention to details and there's passion. Raw, unbridled passion seeping from the canvas. I also remember saying that she's someone who is clearly comfortable with her sexuality, whatever that might be."

"You also said that she probably lived in California, maybe Venus Beach."

Luke turned back to Christina just as she diverted her

gaze to the floor, but he didn't miss the small smile on her lips.

"I always thought you were amazing. Your quiet spirit, your ability to see the positive in any situation, and your sunny personality, but this ..." He waved his hand around the small room, "This is astounding."

A crimson color rose to her cheeks and that shy smile that he had missed like crazy graced her beautiful face. Even with very little makeup, the woman was gorgeous.

"Thank you," she said quietly. "I feel alive when I paint, whether on walls or canvas." She lifted an abstract painting from a drop cloth laid across part of the floor. "I use paint to express myself. When I'm happy, I usually paint landscapes, kids, or animals. When I have a lot on my mind, it's abstract. The darker my mood, the darker the colors."

Again, Luke took in the various paintings strewn around the room, zoning in on the ones that were dramatically dark. It looked as if he hadn't been the only one living the past three months in a dark space. Her mood might have been displayed in her paintings, but he knew another way she expressed herself. He had never been with a sexual partner who was as passionate and free in bed as Christina. One of many aspects of their relationship he missed.

"What do you feel when you paint nudes?" he asked, unable to stop himself.

She thought for a moment. "Passion. Peace. Freedom."

Silence filled the room, both engrossed in their own thoughts. What he didn't understand was why she felt she couldn't tell him about this side of her. Why couldn't she share such an important part of her life with him?

"Why are you hiding behind your talent? Why paint under a pseudonym?"

*

Now for the moment of truth. How would she explain her reasons for keeping a secret? A secret from him as well as her family? Christina didn't know if Luke would ever forgive her deceit, but she had shared this much, she might as well tell him everything.

"Why don't we continue this conversation in the living room?" She moved to the door, her hand hovering over the light switch. Finally, Christina had shared this part of herself with someone other than Jada. It felt good. It felt right.

Again, Luke stood in front of her favorite painting, the one that she would never sell. She wondered if he knew. She wondered if he knew that their time together had inspired the piece.

He turned suddenly and moved toward the door, but stopped short before crossing the threshold. Glancing back, he took one last look before heading back into the living room.

He knew.

"Can I get you something else to drink?" Christina asked and relocked the bedroom door.

"No, I'm good. Thanks." He reclaimed his spot near the window where he stood when they first arrived. She grabbed a bottle of water for herself, noticing his mood had changed. The tension bouncing off of him was undeniable and could be felt clear across the room.

"What I don't understand is why this is a secret." He turned toward her but maintained his distance. "You're a gifted artist. I could see if you were an operative or if you were CIA, but there's no danger of revealing to the world, that you're the talent behind that amazing work."

Pride swelled in her chest. Knowing that he thought she was talented, meant more to her than she ever imagined. Suddenly keeping this part of her life a secret from him didn't seem warranted.

"You don't know the Jenkins family. My grandfather to be more specific." She played with the cap of her water bottle, spinning it on the granite countertop. "Since we were little kids, it has been drilled into us that family comes first. What we do in public or behind closed doors can affect the family. That we shouldn't say or do anything that would cause negative attention on the Jenkins. I don't even want to think about how he would react to my nudes."

"But you only recently started painting nudes."

"I only recently started sharing my nudes with the public. I've been painting them for a while."

"I guess what I'm asking is why didn't you share your work with your family early on, when you were only doing landscapes and abstract?"

"I was afraid my family wouldn't be supportive, wouldn't accept my creativity. They didn't support my father. When he was younger and announced that he wanted to play the drums and the saxophone professionally, he received a lot of pushback from the family. They made comments like – don't quit your day job and keep dreaming. Besides, painting on the side and making a name for myself, feels a little disloyal."

Luke's brows drew together. "How so?"

Christina tried to think of a way to explain what she felt. Luke didn't come from a large family and wouldn't understand the dynamics. "My family has invested a lot into the company, as well as a lot of time and money into me. We work together in one capacity or another to build the Jenkins family brand. To build the Jenkins family empire. That company has been the foundation for all of us as it relates to first jobs. Giving us an opportunity to gain experience, learn a trade and to get further ahead financially than most people our age." She paused thinking about how supportive her family had always been in most aspects of her life. Doing her own thing as an artist, with all of the traveling, as well as her latest shows displaying her nudes, she didn't think this part of her life would go over well.

"I know I only met your family a couple of times, but they seem extremely supportive of each other. I still don't understand your concern."

"I want to tell them, but if they shun my work or think

I'm wasting my time, I don't know if I could take the rejection. Whenever I put a piece out there for sale, I brace myself for the negative feedback. I don't think I could handle it if my family weren't supportive of this." She shrugged. "So I've been keeping this part of my life to myself. Well, actually you and Jada know."

Luke took a deep breath in and released it slowly. When he looked up, their gazes collided. It was as if all the air had been sucked out of the room. The first time they met, there was an immediate attraction and what she saw swimming in his brown eyes now, felt like so much more. Heat spread through her, and every cell tingled as his gaze caressed her like a soft feather.

God she had missed him. She missed everything about him, especially his touch and his deep, toe-curling kisses. Their intellectual conversations from discussing the controversy around one of Robin Thicke's songs to disagreeing about the Affordable Care Act, was something else she missed. Never had she been in such a thoroughly fulfilling relationship than she had when they were together. And their sex life...*whew*. The man made every nerve ending in her body sing. They fit together perfectly in more ways than one.

She wished he would say something.

"You didn't trust me enough to share this part of your life with me."

Okay, maybe she liked it better when he wasn't saying anything. But he was right. Her art was so close to her heart that she wasn't willing to let anyone close to her have a chance of shooting down her dream.

"It wasn't that I didn't trust you."

"Then what was it?"

"I guess I wasn't ready to share this part of my life with anyone. Besides, my family doesn't know. I couldn't see telling someone I was dating about Sasha Knight, before telling them."

"So why now? Why bother telling me, especially if you still haven't told them?"

"I miss you." The words flew out of her mouth before she had a chance to think. After the conversation with Jada, Christina knew that if she wanted another chance with Luke, another chance at love, she had to be straight with him. "Not telling you about this was the biggest mistake I ever made."

He looked away. She wanted another chance with him, but at this point, there was nothing else she could do. Their fate was up to him.

He shoved one hand into his front pocket and rubbed the other hand over his forehead. "For the first time in my life, I don't know what to say. When you refused to tell me why you wanted to stay in New York, I honestly thought you were seeing someone else. I'm glad to know that wasn't the reason, but this new information doesn't excuse the fact that you lied. I opened my heart and my home to you, only to find out you've been lying, keeping something important from me."

Luke might not have come out and said it, but Christina knew part of his reaction had to do with all that he had already lost. He had once told her that one of the reasons he had avoided relationships was because he couldn't stand the thought of losing someone else.

"I'm sorry ... for everything," she moved toward him but stopped when he shook his head and rubbed his eyes.

"I can't help but wonder what other secrets you have. If you were willing to keep something this small from me, how do I know you're not harboring other secrets? Bigger secrets." He glared at her. And just that fast a nice evening had quickly veered south.

"This wasn't a *small* secret." Christina's insides vibrated with anger. "Sasha Knight is a big part of who I am. My creative outlet. All it would take is for one person that I love to belittle what I do, and wipe out any creativity that I have. So forgive me if I held that secret close to my heart. And anyway, I could say the same thing about you keeping secrets."

Confusion showed in his eyes. "Excuse me?"

"You say that you left New York for a quieter, simpler life, but I have a feeling there's more to it. Much more. I've come clean with you. The only way this," she pointed back and forth between them, "is ever going to work is if *we* put everything on the table. No more secrets."

When he didn't respond, Christina had her answer. He was definitely keeping something from her. She walked to the door and opened it.

"Maybe this wasn't a good idea. Good night, Lucas." She used his given name, always preferring it over his nickname.

He hesitated. His eyes were steady on her as seconds ticked by. Finally, he moved toward the door but stopped short.

"Oh and don't worry. Your secret's safe with me."

Christina slammed the door the moment he cleared the threshold.

Asshole.

CHAPTER SEVEN

Days later, Christina pulled into the driveway of Zack and Jada's estate, still pissed at Luke. Her cousin insisted that some retail therapy is what Christina needed to get out of her funk. Unlike Jada, Christina didn't much care for shopping unless it included a trip to a thrift shop or an antique store.

She climbed out of the car and walked along the cobblestone walkway trying to free her mind of Luke. She didn't know why she was still mad at him. It was her fault for withholding information. No, actually, she did have a good reason for still being angry. He acted like a complete jerk the other night. Well, maybe not a complete jerk, but a jerk nonetheless. At first, her heart sang inside her chest at how impressed and complimentary he was of her work, but the way he left was unforgivable. Sure she could understand that he was hurt that she had lied to him. Okay, she had lied more than once, but still. She had a good reason. She wasn't totally confident in her abilities as an artist … yet. She couldn't afford to have anyone, especially him, derail her mission of being a world renowned artist. All it would have taken was for him to say the wrong thing and she might've given up.

"Are you coming in?" Jada stood at the open door, her hands on her hips and a frown covering her ruby red lips. Christina hadn't realized she rang the doorbell or that Jada had opened the door.

She stepped into the house without saying hello or anything else. Instead, she made a beeline to the half-bath off of the family room, slamming the door behind her. The door barely closed before she burst into tears. Normally, she wasn't a crier, but at the moment she felt as if her heart had been ripped from her chest and stomped on over and over again. She hadn't shed this many tears since the day after Luke had left New York. But the other night, she had been more angry than sad, calling him every name but his own.

Letting the lid of the toilet seat down, she sat on it, propped her elbows on her knees and buried her face in her hands. The smell of lavender from the air freshener sitting on the counter should have been calming, but the scent did nothing to make her feel better.

Jada knocked on the door, calling out Christina's name for the first few minutes before she eventually walked away. No sooner than she left, Christina jumped at the loud pounding on the other side of the door.

"CJ?" Zack yelled. "You need to let us know if you're okay otherwise this door is coming down!"

Christina had no doubt that the former football star would plow through the door if Jada asked him to.

"I'm fine. I just need a minute." Christina sighed with resignation. Actually, she needed more than a minute. Days would have been a more accurate estimation.

Fifteen minutes later, she had finally pulled herself together enough to leave the bathroom. She opened the door to find Jada standing in front of it with a container of their favorite butter pecan ice cream. How many nights had she shared a tub of ice cream with Jada? Christina didn't care what anyone said. Butter pecan ice cream was the cure for any ailment.

Jada handed Christina the container, a long handled spoon sticking out of it. "I can't remember the last time I saw you cry and I didn't know what else to do. And don't worry," another spoon miraculously appeared from behind Jada's back, "you won't have to eat alone."

Christina laughed through her tears and accepted the ice cream as well as a hug from her cousin. The small gesture was making her feel better already.

They ate and talked in the family room about practically everything under the sun. The one topic that was off limits though – *Luke*. Jada had made the mistake of mentioning his name during part of the conversation and Christina had abruptly broken into tears again. Granted she knew some of her sadness was from the way things ended the other night, but part of her emotional state was from lack of sleep.

"Jada," Zack called from upstairs. "Can you come here a minute?"

"I'll be right back." Her cousin stood and hurried from the room.

Minutes later the doorbell rang. When Christina didn't hear anyone going to the door, she wondered if Jada or Zack heard the bell.

"CJ, get the door," Jada called out.

On the way down the hall, Christina spotted herself in a mirror and shivered at how puffy and red her eyes were. "Oh great, I look a mess." She rubbed the smeared mascara from under her eyes with the back of her index finger and blinked several times. Despite her efforts, she still looked as if she had spent the last hour crying.

Christina swung the front door open and immediately regretted not looking to see who'd be standing on the other side of it. If only there were a large boulder somewhere that she could hide behind. Seeing Luke, looking good enough to eat, she felt like she was going to start crying all over again.

"What's going on? What happened?" He said in a rush

when he walked into the house, not taking his concerned gaze from her face. His hand went to the back of her neck and pulled her into his chest, holding her tightly. Christina didn't know what the heck was going on, but at the moment, she didn't care.

"You're what happened you idiot!" They both jerked apart to find a scowling Zack standing in the middle of the foyer with Jada close by his side. Christina took a step away from Luke and quickly swiped at a wayward tear crawling down her cheek. "Do you see the tears in her eyes? She looks like that because of your ass." Zack pointed his finger at Luke. "So you need to fix whatever the hell is going on! Now!" Her cousin-in-law snatched his keys from the counter and reached for Jada's hand, pulling her toward the kitchen. Christina didn't miss the Cheshire grin planted on her cousin's lips. "And set the alarm if you leave before we get back."

We've been set up. Her cousin had always been sneaky, but this stunt outshined any of her previous ones.

*

Luke cursed under his breath and wiped his hand slowly over his mouth, letting it rest on his chin. His gaze met Christina's teary eyes and his heart lurched in his chest. Never had she cried in his presence and the thought of him being the cause of her tears tore him up inside. She looked about as bad as he felt. The last two days had been hell. Now he understood why Zack had called him in a fit of rage, telling him that he needed to get over there ASAP because something had happened to her. Luke had never been so scared in his life, thinking the worse.

"Baby, I'm sorry." There was no way he was letting another day go without apologizing for his jacked up attitude the other night and for any other grief he might have caused her. "I could have … no, I should have handled the other night better than I did."

"I'm sorry too. I'm sorry for everything. I don't want to

fight anymore and I swear I'll never lie to you again."

"Me either." Not giving her a chance to say anything else, he lowered his mouth over hers and kissed her with everything he had. Repairing their relationship was going to take more than 'I'm sorry' but an apology was a good start. He didn't know what it would take, but he wanted them to find their way back to each other. He wanted what they once had. He needed what they once had.

Luke lifted his head from hers, still cradling her face between his hands. "We need to talk." He used the four words she had spoken that last night in New York and again when he ran into her a week earlier. The words he hated.

"On one condition."

Fear crept through Luke's body. He didn't like deals or conditions, especially when his heart was involved. "And what's that?"

"We agree never to use those four words again."

Luke shook his head and grinned. "Deal." He was glad to see she still had her sense of humor though her smile seemed a bit sad. Zack was right about him. He was an idiot. He could have ended this nonsense between them the other night, yet he chose to walk away from the only woman he had ever cared about. The only woman he had ever loved.

Staring down into her eyes, Luke caressed her cheeks with the pads of his thumbs. "I love you," he whispered. He had never spoken those words to any other woman. "I love you so frickin' much I feel as if I'm going to lose my damn mind whenever we're apart. I need you in my life, baby. I'm willing to do whatever it takes to make that happen."

She molded against his body, her arms wrapped tightly around him and her head buried in the crook of his neck. He didn't know what else to do but hold her.

She finally looked up at him, tears hanging on her long eyelashes. "I love you too. These last few months have been awful. I didn't think … I never thought I'd hear those words from you."

He wrapped his arms around her again, enjoying the feel of her curves against his body. He placed a lingering kiss against her temple. "I should have told you a long time ago." Then maybe they wouldn't be in this mess. *No more secrets.* Luke didn't know how long they stood in Zack's foyer, but it was time to settle things with Christina once and for all. "Come on, let's get out of here."

An hour later, Luke walked into his condominium carrying Christina, who was asleep in his arms. He had intended for them to talk on the way to his place, which was why he suggested they leave her car at Zack and Jada's house. But she had fallen asleep within minutes of their long drive.

He placed her in the center of his four-poster king-size bed, not bothering to pull the covers back. She was out cold. She didn't even stir when he took her shoes off her feet.

Luke stood back, his hands shoved into the front pockets of his pants and his heart swelled seeing her lying in his bed. He had once admitted to her that he didn't sleep well without her lying next to him. After all this time, that fact still remained true. The thought of sleeping in a bed without her made him physically ill.

Luke pulled his T-shirt over his head, feeling a nap was a good idea. Last night he probably only had a solid two hours of sleep. In the past, much of his insomnia had to do with the high profile cases he took on. There was a time when he could separate himself from that part of his life once he left the office or left the courthouse, but somehow over time, his work became his life. And the last few years the cases became more challenging, and he slept fewer and fewer hours.

Stripping out of his jeans, he tossed them in the clothes hamper in the back of his closet. Normally he wasn't one to sleep in pajamas, but in light of his visitor and the rockiness of their relationship, sleeping in the nude wasn't an option. He grabbed a pair of pajama bottoms from his dresser and slipped into them.

Pulling the extra blanket from the closet, he spread it over Christina before climbing into the bed next to her. As much as he wanted to wake her, if for nothing more than to stare into her eyes, he resisted. Instead, he let his gaze study her face. She appeared so peaceful. Her long eyelashes fanned over her cheeks and that sweet mouth of hers held a slight smile, making him smile too. A nose ring. He reached out and touched the diamond stud, surprised that she'd been daring enough to go through with getting her nose pierced.

Unable to resist, he gently gathered her into his arms, her head resting on his chest. He breathed in and the smell of wildflowers, her usual scent tickled his nose. Peace he hadn't felt in a long time fell over him, lulling him into a deep sleep.

*

Christina slipped into one of Luke's dress shirts and quietly tiptoed out of his bedroom, closing the door behind her. She couldn't believe she had slept over five hours. Luke must have been just as tired because he was normally a light sleeper. She had climbed out of his bed, showered and he hadn't moved. The whole routine brought back memories of happier times.

Quietness except for the soft hum of the air conditioner surrounded her as she eased down the semi-dark hallway. She glanced into a guest room, Luke's office, and a bathroom on route to the main part of the condominium. She now stood in the great room and noticed the sun starting to set through the opened blinds.

Christina didn't see a light switch on any nearby walls, so she headed to a table lamp, bumping the edge of an overstuffed chair along the way. The light emitted a soft glow around the room. From where she stood, she could see the kitchen, a dining room, and a closed door to her left.

She took a slow stroll around the luxury space. Luke's new place was just as neat and extravagant as the one in

New York. He loved the finer things in life, and it showed in his taste in furniture, fixtures and now that she was in the kitchen, appliances.

After a quick glance in the kitchen, Christina went back into the great room. She had never met a man who kept everything so tidy. He had purchased another white pit set that only took up a portion of the square footage, leaving plenty of space to move about easily. The taupe color walls with white trim complimented the décor of browns, sage, and burnt orange sprinkled around the space.

She had two words for the decor – interior designer. Luke might have been a neat freak, but he didn't have the first clue about decorating a home.

Christina froze when a painting on the wall across the room caught her attention. Easing up to the artwork, joy fluttered in her gut and a smile played on her lips. It was one of hers. One of her abstracts. It was one of her earlier pieces. The cool colors blended perfectly with the room design as if specifically made for the space.

It was one thing to see her work hanging on gallery walls or in her own home, but to see one of her paintings displayed in someone else's home excited her in a way she hadn't expected.

She stood staring at the picture trying not to zone in on any flaws, but couldn't stop herself from thinking she should have used a darker blue. Like most artistic people, she had yet to look at one of her pieces and not think about what she could have done differently.

Feeling rested and excited, she turned on her heels and almost did a happy dance back to Luke's bedroom. He had some explaining to do. She wanted to know when, where, and how he'd found one of the first paintings she had ever done.

*

Luke wasn't sure what had awakened him, but when he opened his eyes, Christina was standing near the foot of the bed, leaning against one of the bedpost.

"I hope you don't mind, but I used your shower. And I gave myself a tour of your place."

He lifted his head slightly. His sleepy gaze raked lazily over her from the thick hair tumbled around her shoulders to his dress shirt draping her body. He didn't have to wonder if she had anything on underneath. He knew her. She hated clothes. It was a wonder she had bothered to put on anything. Besides that, he could see her nipples hardened behind the light material.

He groaned at that realization and dropped his head back on the pillow, throwing his forearm over his eyes. Damn his body for reacting. This woman and her enticing body were going to be the death of him.

"Make yourself at home." He wasn't ready to get up. Actually, he wasn't ready for her to get up either. "C'mere. Come back to bed." He held out his other arm and heard her soft steps moving closer to the bed. When his hand met a smooth thigh, he lifted the arm that was covering his eyes and met her gaze.

Not needing any encouragement, she climbed on top of him. When he had asked her to come back to bed, his intentions were good, but now...

She squealed when he flipped her onto her back, her beautiful smile a lot brighter than it had been earlier.

"I hope you're not in a hurry to leave. I have big plans for you." Luke pushed a strand of hair behind her ear.

Pulling his face to hers, Christina kissed him with an intensity that left no doubt to what she wanted and he was just the person to give it to her. Their tongues tangled to a familiar rhythm, reminding him of how much he had missed her taste, missed the feel of her nakedness beneath him. She was right where she was supposed to be. Right there with him. For months, Luke had wondered if he would ever have her in his arms again. Wondered if he would ever get the chance to hold her, touch her, love on her.

"I've missed you," he said when he lifted his head, caressing her cheek. Her freshly showered scent swirled around him, awakening the ardor he had only for her. "You have no idea how I've missed you."

She placed her hand on his jaw and stared into his eyes. "Actually, I do. I love you so much. I promise I never meant to hurt you. Never meant to ruin what we had."

Instead of responding, he covered her mouth with his, nipping at her lower lip, then the top one. "Sweet. So sweet," he mumbled. He slid his hand down the side of her body, appreciating every curve and dip. No bra. No panties. Easy access. Just the way he liked it.

Luke raised up slightly, his elbow holding his weight as he undid the top two buttons on the shirt she wore. Though he loved it when she put on his clothes, he loved it better when she wasn't wearing anything.

His hands went lower. Smoothed, toned skin peeked from behind the twill fabric as he undid yet another button and slowed. Opening the material, a smile crept across his lips. "A nose ring *and* you have your belly-button pierced ... I like." He fingered the diamond hanging from a gold stud. He never knew what to expect from his little seductive vixen, but Christina never disappointed.

Luke glanced up and their gazes collided. His pulse galloped as he stared into clear, dark eyes that held so much love and desire, tugging hard on his heartstrings. He was a goner. One look, one incredibly sexy woman, and a pierced belly button had him falling deeper and unequivocally in love with this woman.

He cleared his throat and returned his attention to the task at hand. "What other treats do you have for me?"

Christina caressed the back of his bare arm that was bracing him up. "Let your gaze and your fingers take you lower..." Her voice trailed off and he did as she suggested.

He arrived at the last button. The button holding together the portion of the shirt that covered the part of her body he couldn't wait to dive into. He unfastened the shirt and let the halves fall open. Warmth spread through his body and his penis leaped to attention.

"Damn, baby." His gaze steadied on the short curls leading to the V between her firm thighs. "You're just full of surprises aren't you?" He ran his hand from her flat abs on down to her pubic hair, formed in a perfect heart-shaped design.

"You have no idea," she said on an unsteady breath, her lower body arching to his touch. Unable to help himself, his fingers went lower, not stopping until he was at the entrance to her core. He entered her with one finger and she whimpered and moved against his hand. *Wet and hot.* "Lu…" Her words hung in the air, her nails digging into his arm.

"You like that?"

"Lu…Lucas don't play with me. You know I do." Her voice held a husky edge as she moved with each thrust of his finger. "Please," she begged. He added another finger, this time going deeper and harder, massaging her interior walls.

Luke captured her lips again, sucking on her tongue as he picked up the pace sliding his digits in and out of her. Hearing her soft moans, a hot tide of lust built within him. Desire pulsated through his veins and straight to his erection. There was no way in hell he'd be able to take this reuniting of their bodies slow with the way her hips lifted higher on the bed, her moves more frantic against his hand. She was close. She was close to her ….

Christina snatched her mouth from his. "Lucas!" Her hips rose fully off the bed bucking and jerking uncontrollably. Her head thrashed against the pillow. "Ohmigod. Ohmigod." She locked her thighs shut and clung to him as she shattered around his hand, her eyes tightly shut.

Not waiting for her to come down off her high, Luke reached over and pulled a condom from the drawer next to the bed. He rid himself of his pajama bottoms and quickly sheathed himself.

"I'm not done with you yet." He nudged her thighs further apart, moving between her legs.

"Good." Her breathing came in short spurts and she smiled up at him, a light sheen across her forehead. "We have some time to make up for and I'm planning on us going all night long."

Luke laughed and positioned himself above her, bracing his hands on each side of her head. "I love how ambitious you are." If anyone could go all night long, it was Christina. Luke had never met a woman with her sexual appetite and stamina.

He trailed kisses from her cheek, down the column of her neck and didn't stop until he reached her breasts. The feel of his tongue swirling around a taut nipple sent lust sweeping through her body like a runaway train barreling down a steep hill. Christina knew she would lose it again soon when he caught the harden peak gently between his teeth, sending a sweet thrill to the soles of her feet.

"Baby, I need you inside me." She wiggled beneath him and placed her hands on the side of his face, getting his attention. Her nipple popped out of his mouth and he grinned up at her.

"Impatient are we?"

"Yes." She pulled him to her and kissed him with a hunger that let him know just how her impatience had grown to explosive proportions. She loved that he liked to take his time making love, but her sex throbbed for him, longed for what she'd been missing.

Luke gripped her left butt cheek, lifting her hip slightly off the bed as he slowly entered her moist opening, sending erotic jolts of pleasure to every nerve in her body. Christina held the back of his head firmly, increasing the pressure of his kiss as their bodies rocked in harmony. *Just like old times.*

Luke moaned against her lips as he plunged deeper, and

harder, picking up the pace with each thrust. Christina rotated her hips and grasped his butt, feeling him grow thicker inside her. She squeezed her thighs around him as adrenaline coursed through her veins. This is what she wanted, what she had missed.

"Chri...stina," he growled when he yanked his lips from hers. Fierce hunger lurked in his eyes as his stiff shaft pounded in and out of her with such force, she could barely hold on to his sweat slicked shoulders.

Christina bit down on her bottom lip as she held his intense gaze, matching him stroke for stroke. But with the pressure building in her core, there was no way she could hold on much longer. No sooner as the thought entered her mind, Luke hit the spot that always pushed her over the edge.

She cursed under her breath and slammed her eyes shut. Her arms flung out and she fisted the sheets as her heart hammered and a frenzy of pleasure shot through her core. Christina couldn't hold on. Luke's name flew from her lips and an orgasm rippled through her body like a seismic sea wave washing out everything in its way.

Luke's moves grew more frantic and with one final thrust, his body stiffened and he roared her name before collapsing on top of her. Panting hard, they lay that way, shivering in each other's arms, struggling to catch their breath.

Minutes ticked by, neither mumbled a word. So many emotions bounce inside of Christina as she marveled at the peace that had washed over her. She had dreamed, hoped for this moment for months, not knowing whether they would ever be joined together again. And here they were.

"God I've missed you," she whispered into the quietness of the room.

Luke lifted his head and kissed her sweetly. "Not as much as I've missed you."

*

"Lucas?"

"Hmm?" Luke didn't open his eyes. As long as she was curled up next to him, her smooth legs intertwined with his lounging on the bed, all was well in his world. Besides, over the last two hours she had worn his ass out. "I've missed hearing you call me that."

"When you're dressed in your expensive suits, designer ties, and shoes so shiny I can see myself, the name Lucas fits you better than Luke."

"But at the moment, I'm not wearing a suit, tie, or shoes." He turned his head to look at her, fatigue keeping him from opening his eyes completely.

She grinned. "Funny." Mischief shimmered in her eyes, as her gaze remained steady on him. He had no idea what she was thinking, but he could look at her all day lo…

"*Shit*," he gasped and practically leaped off the bed when her cold hands wrapped around his shaft. He slammed his eyes closed and cursed under his breath when her grip tightened. They had already gone three rounds and for the first time in his life, he was going to have to turn her down if she insisted on another go at it.

He slid his hand beneath the sheet and covered her hand. "Are you trying to kill me?" he asked through gritted teeth.

That wicked little grin she flashed whenever she was up to no good, slid across her lips. "Are you saying that you can't hang?"

"That's exactly what I'm saying." She laughed and loosened her grip, but didn't remove her hand completely. "I'm not proud of it, but I'm a little out of practice."

That seemed to get her attention. During their separation, no other woman held his attention long enough to want to talk her out of her panties. That's because this beautiful woman staring down at him now had his heart.

"I'm glad you're out of practice," she said softly and climbed on top of him, kissing him with so much passion. At that moment, she could ask for anything and he'd try to deliver. Though he didn't think he had another round in him, the way she was making love to his mouth was sure to get a rise out of him.

"Mmm, Christina," he mumbled against her lips.

She lifted her head and smiled. "Lucas," she spoke his given name again as if testing it out on her tongue.

Before his mother died, she was the only person who called him Lucas. He had to admit, he liked when Christina called him by his given name.

"My mother would have loved you," he said pushing her hair away from her face, relishing how silky soft it felt between his fingers. "I don't remember everything about her, but in some ways you remind me of her."

Christina caressed his cheek. "In what ways?"

Luke's mother had died of ovarian cancer. Watching her day after day, fight the disease, enduring chemotherapy and then radiation, took its toll on her, as well as him and his father. Since they didn't have much family, once she was gone, his whole world had changed. It was one of the loneliest times of his life.

"She was really sweet and smiled a lot. Everyone who knew her loved her." He placed a lingering kiss against Christina's cheek. He wasn't sure why, but he'd been thinking about his mother more lately. "She did so much for others. Buying groceries, giving folks money to get their lights turned back on. Whatever people needed, she was there for them. It's not that she and my dad had much money, but the little they had, she used to help others. I often told her that I was going to make a lot of money so that she wouldn't have to use her money to help others."

"I know she's looking down on you, proud of the man you've become."

He could only hope. There were so many things he had done over the years that he wasn't proud of. Things he wished he could do over. Then maybe he would be more confident that his mother was proud of the man he had become.

"You were right about me having another reason for leaving New York." Christina lifted her head from his chest and met his gaze. When he didn't continue, she climbed off of him and reclaimed her space on the bed next to him, as if sensing his discomfort in what he was about to tell her. She pulled the sheet up higher over her naked body and propped up on her elbow.

When he didn't speak right away, she said, "If you're not ready to tell me, I understand. Look how long it took me to tell you about Sasha Knight."

"I had a brother." He twirled a lock of her hair around his finger.

She lifted a perfectly arched eyebrow. "Had?"

He nodded. "My half brother. My father had an affair about a year after I was born. I don't know all the details, but while I was in my sophomore year of high school, I found out about him."

"How did you find out?"

Luke turned onto his back and stared up at the ceiling, his hand caressing Christina's smooth thigh. She was soft in all the right places and he felt a sense of calm fall upon him whenever his hands were on her.

"We attended the same high school," he finally said. He told her how some of his classmates had mentioned that there was a guy who favored him in their classes. After a few weeks of hearing this from different people, he finally met Scott. They had different last names, but the resemblance was strong. It turned out that his father didn't even know Scott existed.

"That had to be wild. Did you guys become friends?"

"Not really. We were friendly, but we didn't hang out. Scott ran with a different crowd. A group of guys that were bad news and spent more time on the streets than they did in school. My father wasn't having that with me. After my mother had died, he rode my ass to get good grades, saying she wanted me to be a doctor or a lawyer. Now, I'm glad my dad stayed on me, but back then, I hated him for it. I couldn't catch a break with the old man. B's weren't good enough. I had to bring home A's or he'd beat my ass."

"What about Scott? Did your father have a relationship with him?"

Luke shook his head. "Nah. He tried, but Scott wasn't interested. They didn't hate each other, but since neither of them knew about the other until Scott was almost grown, they never did establish a bond."

Christina moved closer. Luke wrapped his arm around her, his hand resting on her hip, her head near his shoulder just under his chin.

"That's so sad. I can't imagine my parents not being in my life. I'm surprised Scott's mother didn't insist on child support or something. How is it that your father didn't know about him?"

"From what I understand, it was a one-time thing with my father and Scott's mother. Supposedly, she wanted a child, without the husband. Though according to my father, he didn't know that. They worked on a committee together for months and then attended a conference in Boston," Luke shrugged, "one thing led to another and they had a one night stand."

Christina didn't say anything for a while, her soft touch on his chest was so relaxing, and he struggled to keep his eyes open. He wished they could just stay like that - in bed, together, surrounded by silence, but there was more to tell.

"What does Scott have to do with you leaving New York?" she asked as if reading Luke's mind.

"He's dead."

She sat upright. "Oh my God." One of her hands hovered over her mouth, the other over her heart. "When? How?" Her eyes as wide as saucers, she moved away from him.

Maybe he shouldn't have just blurted out that part.

"Come here." He tried pulling her back down, but she

wouldn't budge.

"What does Scott being dead have to do with you being in Cincinnati, Lucas?"

It wasn't until she leaned further away from him did he realize what she must have been thinking. Now he was sitting up, the sheet tangled around him.

"I know you don't think I had anything to do with his death," he said in a tone rougher than intended, causing her to scoot back more. Swallowing hard, he tried to rein in his anger. "I had nothing to do with his death, CJ." He stood, and stepped into his pajama bottoms. Walking over to the window, his back to her, he took a moment to slow his breathing.

"Then ... then what happened?"

Luke turned to her. She was standing next to the bed with the sheet wrapped around her curvaceous figure. Her tousled hair making her look as desirable as if she was all dressed up and in full makeup.

"He got into some trouble about eight months ago and was up on murder charges. He asked me to defend him." Luke breathed in and released the breath slowly as he turned back to the window looking out at nothing in particular. "The judge set bail at a million dollars."

Luke startled when Christina placed her hand on his back. He hadn't heard her approach.

"And?"

His throat tightened and a gut-wrenching ache had him rubbing his stomach. He felt sick just thinking about that day. Based on his initial interview with his brother, Luke knew he was guilty but agreed to defend him. He had to. They were brothers.

Luke thought he could keep his brother safe by having him sit in jail for a little while, thinking Scott couldn't come up with the million dollar bail. All Luke needed was a little more time. At least long enough to cut a deal and get Scott put into the government's witness protection program if he agreed to testify against the capofamiglia - the boss of the Donati family.

"Lucas?"

"Someone posted his bail before I was notified. There was a hit out on Scott. He was dead within an hour of being released."

"Oh. My. God. I'm so sorry." Her arms went around Luke's waist and she laid her head against his back, holding him tight.

He hadn't planned to share anything about their relationship. Only his friend, a P.I and Zack knew that they were brothers. And now, Christina.

During high school, neither he nor Scott were interested or willing to claim each other publically. And when Luke went to California to school, they had lost contact. He didn't even know his brother knew how to reach him until Luke had received a call from him at three o'clock one morning. Scott was in jail.

Christina lifted her head and loosened her grip, stepping to the side of Luke. He glanced down at her, not missing the tears misting her eyes. She had such a sweet, gentle spirit. Here she was getting emotional for a man she didn't even know. A man who had lived his life on the streets of New York doing God knows what.

"Are you ... are you in danger? Is that why you moved here?" She visibly shivered and he pulled her close hoping to comfort her.

"No. I moved here because of all of the loss and shit I experienced in New York. Between working so many crazy hours, losing my family over the years and the type of cases I was getting ... it was starting to be too much. I was defending people, some I knew were guilty." He shrugged. "I just couldn't do it anymore. I didn't *want* to do it anymore. I needed a new start. I needed to regroup. Zack suggested Cincinnati."

"What about the stuff Scott was caught up in?"

"I have friends in high and low places who keep me informed. Looks like Scott might have been set up to take the fall for someone in one of the largest crime families in New York. I never had a chance to dig into the case. After he was killed, I didn't think it was safe for me to pursue answers."

"So I don't have to worry about something happening to you? You're not going to try to retaliate?"

He had done plenty of stupid stuff over the years but trying to kill off a crime family wouldn't make the list.

"No to both questions. From what we can tell, no one knows that Scott and I were brothers."

"What about his mother?"

"She was killed in a car accident last year. Being parentless was the one thing we had in common." The bitterness in his mouth seeped out with each word, threatening to consume him the way it had when he found out his brother had been killed. He and Scott might not have been close, but they were family. Everyone Luke ever cared about had been snatched from him in some way.

Luke wrapped his arms around Christina and held her tight. He didn't think he could handle losing anyone else, especially her.

CHAPTER EIGHT

Christina snuggled closer to Luke, reveling in his body heat. Back together for a month, it was as if they had never split. They had fallen into a good routine and she planned to do whatever she could to never feel the emptiness that she felt when they broke up, which seemed like a lifetime ago.

"What are you thinking about?" Luke turned onto his side and draped his arm across her waist, pulling her to his body.

"I was thinking how glad I am that we're back together." She ran her fingers through the barely there hairs on his chest. "I missed this, lounging around on a Saturday morning sharing pillow talk."

Seconds passed without him speaking, his fingers sifting through her hair, something he often did. When he looked at her, the way he was doing now with such intensity, the love she had for him bubbled inside of her, making her giddy like a schoolgirl.

"After my mother died, I never let anyone else get close to me, close to my heart, not even my father." He lifted her chin, forcing their eyes to meet. "You're everything I never knew I needed. Never knew I wanted. You're compassionate, creative and your loving touch keeps me thinking about you throughout the day."

"Aw, that's so sweet."

"But you know what I love most about you?"

"No. What?"

"You're a freak."

"What?" Christina laughed and pounded on his chest. "I can't believe you said that! Why'd you have to ruin the moment?"

"Quit," he said laughing, blocking her swats. "Why are you hitting me? You know you're a freak." They wrestled before he halted her moves by pinning her to the bed and then he turned serious. Staring into her eyes, his fingers gently caressed her cheek. "But you're my freak, and baby I wouldn't have you any other way. You're the best thing that's ever happened to me. And that's on the real."

For the next hour, they talked and laughed. Christina couldn't remember ever being as happy as she was at that moment. Glad the secrets were behind them, she wished they had talked, really talked before she allowed her half-truths to almost ruin their relationship.

They finally got out of bed, showered, and were in Luke's kitchen eating breakfast. He had cleaned the kitchen as he cooked and Christina marveled at how different they were when it came to housekeeping. Luke was ridiculously neat and her ... not so much.

"Tomorrow for Sunday brunch, my family is having a cook out at my grandparent's house. You want to go with me?" The last two times she had asked him to Sunday brunch he turned her down. He had spent time with some of her male cousins, but Luke was an important part of her life. She wanted him to get to know everyone else and for everyone to get to know him.

He watched her over the rim of his coffee cup.

"What?" She shrugged, wondering what was going through his mind.

He set his mug on the round glass table. They were sitting

near the window overlooking a swimming pool.

"So why do you guys have to get together every week? What if you want to do something else like, oh I don't know, cook dinner here?"

"Then I would cook dinner here. We get together weekly because that's what families do." She pushed her plate aside and leaned forward. "Where is this coming from? Do you have a problem with my family?"

He shook his head. "Nah. I don't have a problem with them."

"Then what's with the questions? And why do you keep turning down the invite?"

Luke stared down at the mug in front of him, steam billowing from the dark liquid. How could he tell her that he didn't do family gatherings? That he didn't want to get close to her family and he didn't want them to get close to him? He already felt vulnerable letting Christina get so close. Now she wanted him to welcome her family into his world.

"I think your family is cool, but I'm just not into the lovey-dovey, let's get together every week scene. I get this is what you guys do, but you have to understand. That's not who I am."

"That's nonsense. We both know why you don't want to get close to others. But let me explain something to—"

"Christina, baby, let's not do this." He stood abruptly with his coffee mug, his chair scraping across the travertine floor. His hasty retreat to the coffee pot across the kitchen confirmed what she suspected.

"Let's not do what, *Lucas*? You don't want me to call you out on your fear of letting anyone get close to you? Or is it that you don't want to get close to anyone for fear of one day losing them? Which is it?"

He refilled his mug without responding. She didn't miss the way his jaw clenched or the death grip he had on the handle of the coffee pot. Maybe she needed to try a different approach.

"I can't even imagine what it's like to not have a family to call on in the time of trouble. Or a family that doesn't butt in when you don't want them to. But I do know what it feels like to laugh and joke with people who love you. Or how it feels to have someone be there to hold you up when your heart breaks or your knees go weak." She thought of Jada and the way she and Zack rallied to get her and Luke back together.

Luke turned and faced her, his back leaning against the counter. "Can't you accept that I just might not want to be around a lot of people tomorrow?"

"No." She stood and approached him. "There will be times when we don't want to do something that the other wants to do or go someplace the other wants to go. But if you asked me to go *anywhere* with you. Do you know what I'd do?" When he didn't respond, she continued. "I'd go. Do you know why?" Still no response. "Because I love you. That's what people who love each other do. And I love you so damn much at times if feels as if my heart is going to explode."

"Christina."

"I'm inviting you because I want you there with me." She felt herself getting choked up but refused to let any tears fall. "No, I don't expect you to be all lovey-dovey with my family. Or automatically fall in love with them. What I want is for you to try to get to know them because they're important to me. I know they can be intimidating, but ..."

"Stop." Luke set his mug on the counter and grabbed hold of her hand, pulling her against his body. "Just stop. There is nothing I won't do for you. Understand? If attending the brunch means this much to you, consider it done. You're right. Letting others into my world doesn't come easy, but I understand how important your family is to you. I will try to be more ... social. Just don't cry. I can't handle seeing you cry."

Christina wrapped her arms around his waist and laid her

head against his chest. Hearing his heart beat wildly against her ear, she should have felt guilty for forcing him to go with her, but she didn't. No way would she let him close himself off because of fear of getting too close to others. He deserved to experience what it was like to have a close family love on him. And the Jenkins' were just the people to show him what that was like.

*

"Damn man. Is there anything you're not good at?" Christina's cousin, Ben Jr. asked as Luke leaned over the pool table preparing to hit the eight ball into the left corner pocket. "I let you beat me in air hockey, but here you are wiping me out in ping pong and pool." BJ was a painter who often worked with Christina and the biggest competitor of tabletop games from what Luke could tell. They had met a few weeks ago at a bar for a man's night out that Zack had pulled together. Like then, they all got along well, dishing out nonsense and were having a good time.

Luke laughed when BJ groaned as the eight ball tapped the sidewall of the pocket before falling in. He and Christina had arrived at her grandparents' home over an hour ago and he had to admit that he was having a good time with her cousins and her brother. Not having family, he could now see what he had been missing – the jokes, the laughs, and even a serious moment when BJ asked the fellas' advice on dealing with his baby's momma.

"BJ, don't even bother playing Luke in basketball. He's good at that too and will have no mercy when he dunks on your ass," Zack said when he came up behind Luke, slapping him on the shoulder. "He's been this way since college. Unlike some people who lose their talents as they get older, he seems to get better."

"Zack, you should have given a warning before you introduced him to us," Jerry, Christina's brother, chimed in. "I lost twenty bucks to Luke when we played pool at Terrance's bar a few weeks back."

Six years younger than Christina, Jerry was six-two, over two hundred pounds and looked as if he should've been on a football field blocking for a quarterback instead of being a fifth-year electrician apprentice.

"Well, that's better than the forty dollars I lost playing poker with him the other night," Craig Logan, Toni's husband said.

Luke laughed and accepted the moans and groans of how he had beat the cousins and walked away with their money. He had inherited his father's competitive nature and ability to excel at almost anything he attempted. Back in college, Luke's skills had served him well as he often had to hustle up extra cash for things his scholarship hadn't covered.

He put the cue stick back in the rack and grabbed his baseball cap, shoving it on his head low over his eyes. "I'm going to give you fellas some time to practice while I go for a second round of food."

"Whatever, man. Maybe you should just stay up there," BJ said as he racked the pool table, preparing to play the next person.

Luke walked upstairs and outside to the backyard for another plate of food. From where he stood near the deck, he could see Christina and her sister arguing again near the food tables. When he and Christina arrived, Peyton had laid into her for not getting there early to help with the setup. Her sister had shot him the evil eye and he was pretty sure part of the problem between the sisters had to do with him.

They were so into their conversation, they didn't notice a woman lingering near the table listening to them. For the most part, no one else seemed to notice their heated discussion. Children were running around playing. Christina's parents, as well as another couple, were on the makeshift dance floor dancing near the table that held a sound system and speakers. And everyone else sat at tables eating and laughing, enjoying their own conversations.

Luke's attention returned to Christina and her sister as he

slowly approached them.

"You came late with your man and now you're sitting around as if you're an invited guest," Peyton said and set a fruit platter on the table next to the vegetable tray. "I shouldn't have to be the one who always has to set up and then clean up around here."

"PJ, you're really starting to get on my nerves. You've been on my case since we arrived. If there's something wrong and I'm not talking about the brunch, you need to just say it so we can move on." Christina looked up at that moment and smiled when she saw Luke. "Hey there. I was getting ready to search you out to see if you wanted something else to eat." She approached him, planting a sweet kiss on his lips.

He didn't miss Peyton's boy-toy comment and though Christina was smiling, the smile didn't reach her eyes. "What's going on with you and your sister?" He grabbed a couple of pieces of barbecue chicken and ribs. When Christina told him her uncle Martin could burn on the grill, she wasn't kidding. This had to be the best barbecue Luke had ever tasted.

"Nothing." Christina's gaze followed her sister's retreating back as Peyton stomped off to the house. "She has a bug up her butt about something. Instead of telling me what her problem is, she's harassing me about missing the last couple of brunches and claims I'm not much help today." Christina followed behind him, making a plate full of vegetables for herself.

"Does she have an issue with you dating me?" Luke asked the question quietly when two people he didn't know walked past.

Christina's hand hovered over the dinner rolls and she shot him a quick glance. "Wh … why would you say that?" She grabbed the roll and looked everywhere but at him.

"Just a hunch. So why don't you tell me what the problem is. I have a feeling you already know."

Christina sighed and added a spoonful of potato salad to her plate as well as his.

"I'm not really sure. She's been acting strange for months and seems to be taking her issues out on everyone around her."

"So she doesn't have a problem with me or us dating?"

Luke followed Christina over to an empty picnic table set up under an oak tree. He was glad to see it unoccupied since none of the other tables were available.

"She might've mentioned that she thinks you're a bad influence on me."

"How so? She doesn't even know me." Luke had stopped caring a long time ago what people thought of him, but if Peyton was giving Christina a hard time because of him, it was time to nip it in the bud.

"She thinks my piercings and the fact that I don't bend to her every command has something to do with me dating you."

"And does it?" Luke bit into his chicken, savoring the tangy heat and stopped short of licking his fingers.

"Maybe."

"And how do you feel about that?"

Luke had noticed some subtle changes in Christina since they first met, but he liked the changes. Gone was the goody-two-shoe, girl next door type who dressed simply and tried to be everything to everybody. Christina was still sweet, but now she was edgier in her style of dress, the music she listened to, as well as the way she spoke. She cursed more than he remembered, which was probably because of his potty mouth, but she seemed happier, freer.

"I feel great. I love the new me. Well, actually, I don't think it's the new me. I think I have finally come into my own and I'm more comfortable with myself."

"Well, for what it's worth," he scooted closer and nuzzled her scented neck, "I love everything about you."

*

Christina was still grinning when she walked into her grandmother's newly remodeled state-of-the-art kitchen. Luke always knew just the right thing to say to make her feel good. Reiterating how much he loved her was an added bonus.

"Hey Gram, we're running low on potato salad and dinner rolls. Do we have more?" Christina set the semi-empty glass bowl on the dark granite counter.

"We're also out of baked beans," Violet, Christina's mother said when she walked in carrying a long aluminum pan.

"Okay, there's more potato salad in the refrigerator, but we're going to have to make more baked beans."

"I can whip up a batch real quick."

"No!" Christina and her grandmother said in unison. Christina fell out laughing at her mother's facial expression.

Violet placed her hands on her hips and scowled at Christina. "What's wrong with my baked beans? Your daddy loves them."

"That's probably true, Vee, but I was already planning to make some more," Katherine Jenkins said. "But since you're in here, can you slice up the coconut pineapple cake and that chocolate marble cake that I just finished frosting?"

Christina almost burst out laughing at how cool her grandmother handled what could have been a messy situation. Katherine Jenkins was remarkable in dealing with people. She could diffuse practically any type of problem before it happened.

Christina removed the other bowl of potato salad from the refrigerator. She thought her mother was the most amazing woman she knew, but Violet was a horrible cook. Unfortunately, her mother didn't know just how bad of a cook she was since Christina's father ate anything she made as if it were the best thing he ever tasted.

"Okay, let me run to the bathroom. I'll be right back."

"You handled that well," Christina whispered, standing

next to her grandmother. "Then again, maybe it's time you told her that she doesn't know how to cook. She clearly hasn't taken the hint from anyone else."

Her grandmother chuckled. "Bless her heart. Vee is a doll. Even after months of giving her cooking lessons before she and your daddy were married, I don't think she grasped any of what I taught her."

"Is that why you were so adamant about me and Peyton learning to cook?"

"Yes. There was no way I'd have the next generation of girls not knowing how to prepare a decent meal. Besides, someone had to know how to cook in that house."

Christina took the bowl of potato outside. Her grandmother had taught her, Peyton, Toni, Martina and Jada how to cook. As each one of them turned seven, she would have them over to her house for cooking lessons twice a month. Christina and Toni enjoyed it more than the others, especially their baking lessons and the monthly Gramma/granddaughter breakfasts. As they grew older, their relationship with their grandmother grew stronger. For Toni and Martina, their relationship with their grandmother was even tighter since both of them didn't have strong relationships with their mothers.

"We missed you here last Sunday," her grandmother said when Christina walked back into the kitchen.

"Luke and I went away for the weekend."

"I see."

Christina groaned inside. Usually "I see" meant that she really didn't see, or that she wanted to say more.

"Okay, I'm back. I had to let hubby know where I'd be." Violet floated into the kitchen. Christina couldn't help but think of the phrase, *a breath of fresh air,* whenever her mother entered a room. Always smiling with a kind word for everyone she met. Violet Jenkins could light up the darkest room. "Is this platter okay for the coconut pineapple cake?" She held up an oval glass dish.

"Perfect. And CJ, why don't you frost that cake on the counter next to the stove. Use this buttercream frosting." She pointed to two containers of frosting near where her mother was working.

The three of them worked in a comfortable silence. Christina loved moments like this when she could spend time with the most important women in her life. She felt so blessed to have not only one strong, confident, older woman to guide her, but two.

"So what do you guys think of Luke?" she asked adding frosting to the second layer of the three-layer cake.

"Question is what do you think of him?" Her grandmother added brown sugar to the pan of baked beans.

Christina wasn't surprised by the question. Katherine often answered a question with a question. Anything to get them talking.

"He's the most incredible man I have ever met. I'm in love with him."

"Aw, honey, I'm so happy for you." Her mother wrapped her arms around Christina and kissed her on the cheek. Christina didn't think she would ever get tired of her mother's hugs. "I like him too! He's good-looking, intelligent, and have you noticed that he has a sexy walk just like President Obama?"

Christina threw her head back and laughed. Leave it to her mother to notice Luke's walk. God only knows what else she had noticed.

Violet put the dirty, empty cake plates in the farmhouse sink and rinsed her hands. "I know you were pretty upset when you guys broke up, but your relationship seems stronger than ever. I also can't help but notice that your aura is in full bloom now that you two are back together." Violet closed her eyes and held her arms up as if praying. "I can so see you guys making beautiful music, and beautiful babies together."

Christina's mouth dropped open and she watched her

mother walk, no glide out of the room with one of the platters of cake, her long patchwork skirt dragging the floor. Violet always said what was on her mind, which was fine with Christina. She just never knew what would come out of her mother's mouth.

Christina turned to her grandmother frowning. "What does 'your aura is in full bloom' even mean?"

Her grandmother shook her head laughing. "Chile, your guess is as good as mine. That mother of yours know she's special."

"Yeah, that's a nice way of putting it. I'm afraid to ask what you thought of her when daddy first brought her home to meet you and Grampa."

That got another laugh out of her grandmother. "Let's just say, I thought she was special then too." They both laughed and then her grandmother turned serious. "To be honest, though she was different than what I had in mind for your father, I thought she was perfect for him."

"Really?" This was the first time they had a conversation about her parents meeting. "Why did you think she was perfect for him?"

"Growing up, your dad was always very serious and a little stiff if you ask me." Her grandmother smiled as if thinking about a particular instance. "But when Vee came into his life, it was as if someone turned on a switch inside of him. He was like a different person. He laughed more. He started hanging out with his friends more often, whereas before Vee, he stayed in the house watching television or just lying around. He also joined a rock band, spiked hair and all."

"What?" Christina knew her father played the drums and tinkered a little with the sax, but she didn't know he actually joined a band. She had heard that he never fully pursued a career in music the way he wanted to because her uncles and grandfather talked him out of it.

"Your father nearly drove me crazy when he first started

learning how to play the drums. Our house was much smaller back then. So your grandfather made him play out in the garage."

"What else?" Now Christina wanted to know everything.

"Once he started dating your mother, it was as if he gave himself permission to relax and be himself. He even got caught sneaking in through a window one night after missing curfew. Before Vee, he would have never tried anything like that. He wanted to be what he thought your grandfather and I wanted him to be. What I remember most is that he was happier, especially whenever your mother was around. Somewhat like you are when you and Luke are together."

"Really, Gram?"

"Really. I watch you from a distance and your whole face lights up when you see him or whenever he speaks. I'm a true believer that God has the perfect mate for each of us and I think you and your father found yours."

Christina wasn't sure what to say, especially when she thought about her conversation with Peyton. Her sister might've thought Luke was a bad influence, but Christina knew better.

"I thought you didn't like Luke."

Her grandmother set the spoon down on the counter, wiping her hands on her apron. "Why would you think that?"

Peyton was on the tip of her tongue, but instead she said, "I don't know. I guess I just thought—"

"I don't dislike, Luke. I don't know him. He's been over here what, one or two times? And when he is here, he's usually hanging out with Craig, Zack or the other boys." Her grandmother studied her for a moment, her hands on her rounded hips. "Now do you care to tell me what this is all about?"

Christina set the spatula down. She ripped a paper towel from the holder sitting on the counter and wiped her hands.

"You seem to treat Luke differently than you treat Craig and Zack. When they walk into the house, your eyes light up and you turn your cheek up, expecting a kiss from them. You don't do that with Luke." Christina leaned her back against the counter. "But you're right. You haven't really had a chance to get to know him like you have the others. So I guess we'll have to make sure we don't miss many more Sunday brunches."

"Does he have family in Cincinnati?"

"No. He doesn't have any family." Christina's heart hurt for him. She couldn't imagine a life without her family. She told her grandmother how his parents had died, but didn't mention that he had a sibling.

"Well, I'm glad he has you and now he has us. But I'll tell you like I told your other cousins. As long as he treats you right and respects you, he'll always be welcomed in our home."

Hours later, Christina dried the last pot with a sigh of relief. Every Sunday the women took turns with clean up duty. Today it was Christina, Peyton, and Martina's turn, but as usual, Martina found a way to do just a little to claim that she helped and then she disappeared.

"Alright, I'm out of here. See you tomorrow," Peyton said on her way out of the kitchen. At least they were on speaking terms, but there was still some underlying tension between them. Jada said Peyton was probably jealous of Christina's relationship, but Christina wasn't sure that was true. Something else was going on with her sister.

"Hey, baby. You almost ready to go?" Luke walked up behind her and placed a kiss near her ear, the warmth of his breath sending a sweet thrill through her body.

"Perfect timing." She turned to face him, wrapping her arms around his neck. "Has everyone else left?"

Luke shook his head. "Not quite. I just finished playing pool with Jerry and there are a few people still downstairs playing Spades."

"Oh, that'll probably go on for another two hours." Christina stepped out of Luke's arms and grabbed her handbag from the lower shelf in the pantry. "Let me just say bye to my grandparents. Hopefully, they're not upstairs changing clothes yet."

Christina and Luke headed toward the front of the house hand in hand and ran into her grandfather on the way to the door.

"Hey, kids. Are you two leaving?" he asked over his shoulder.

"In a few minutes. We just wanted to say bye to you and Gram before we left."

"Okay, give me a second. This is Walter at the door. He has a piece of art that he's insisting I see before your grandmother and I leave."

"Oh, cool. Maybe I'll check it out too." Christina was drawn to art like ants to sugar. She couldn't resist sticking around to see what new piece her grandfather's friend had found. Walter wasn't an art broker, but he and her grandfather were art enthusiasts.

"You don't mind do you?" Christina whispered close to Luke's ear.

"Nope. Today my time belongs to you. If this is how you want to spend it, looking at art instead of making love to your man, then…" He flashed that sexy grin and wiggled his eyebrows.

"Ohhh. In that case, give me ten minutes and then we're out of here."

"Alright, Walt, let's make this quick," her grandfather said by way of greeting when he opened the front door. He and Walter were the best of friends, growing up together in Arkansas before later moving to Ohio.

"Hey Uncle, Walter." Christina wrapped her arms around his frail shoulders. He was tall like her grandfather but seemed to get thinner as he aged.

"Good seeing you, sweetheart."

Christina was pretty sure he didn't know which granddaughter she was and always went the safe route in referring to all of them as sweetheart. She introduced him to Luke.

"Nice meeting you young man."

"Same here, sir." Luke shook Walter's hand.

"Okay, Walt. Show me what you have there."

Christina and Luke followed them into her grandfather's office, her favorite room in the house. She always felt at home when she stepped into the room, the smell of leather and sandalwood greeting her at the door. The large space with wall-to-wall bookshelves and huge leather furniture brought back fond memories of when she and her cousins used to play in the office.

"Steven, you have to take a look at this. I almost fell over when I found this on eBay. It cost a pretty penny, but I think when you see it, you'll agree that this masterpiece is worth every single cent."

"You said it's a landscape?" Her grandfather asked and pulled a foldaway easel from next to one of the bookshelves while Walter struggled to remove the painting out of the sheath.

"Yes. Do you remember the creek in Arkansas where we all used to fish?" Walter asked.

"Of course. It's my favorite spot in the world. That's where I asked my Katherine to marry me, right under that huge elm tree."

The small hairs on the back of Christina's neck stood at attention. She unconsciously took a step back as tension spun in her gut.

It couldn't be.

CHAPTER NINE

As if sensing Christina's distress, Luke moved closer, his arm slid around her waist. "You okay?" His words were quiet, meant for her ears only.

All Christina could do was nod, her focus trained on the painting that was still covered. She didn't want to jump to conclusions, but a sinking feeling lodged in her chest as she struggled to breathe.

It was as if Walter removed the covering in slow motion and then there it was. Her first sell. The painting that had landed her an agent.

All the air seemed to seep from the room and her knees went weak. If it weren't for Luke holding her up, Christina was sure she would have puddled to the floor.

Her grandfather stood opened mouth, gaping at the picture. "Who's the artist?" he finally asked.

"Sasha something or another." Walter put on his glasses and pulled a sheet of paper from his wallet. "Oh, here we go. The artist is Sasha Knight."

How in the world did he find this?

"Never heard of her, but if the rest of her work is anything like this ..." Steven Jenkins' voice trailed off as he continued staring at the painting and then he turned to Christina. "Do you remember when I used to tell you and your cousins stories about the creek?"

Perspiration laced Christina's top lip and her heart beat double time. All she could do was nod, not trusting herself to say anything.

"I told you this was a piece that you had to see." Walter straightened the painting on the easel as both he and her grandfather studied the art.

"The details are unbelievable. I had a photo, but it disappeared years ago. I wish I still had it because this painting is almost identical, even down to the daffodils along the water's edge." Christina didn't miss the wistfulness in her grandfather's voice. He had always been full of stories of his childhood, but the creek held so many fond memories of his youth.

Guilt stabbed Christina in the gut for borrowing the photo without telling him and then not returning it. That was her first landscape painting. She had entered it into a contest not thinking it would be the painting to jumpstart her career.

She could feel Luke's gaze on her as she tuned in and out of her grandfather and Walter's conversation.

"Baby, this is a perfect opportunity to tell him. I'm right here with you."

Of course, he was right, but …

"Steven?" Her grandmother's voice carried from the hallway. "You're going to make us late," she said walking into the room wearing a sleek navy blue dress with low heels. "Oh, hi Walter. I should have known you were the one holding him up."

Walter grinned and kissed her on the cheek. "Hey, Katy. This old coot would have probably been down here putzing around whether I was here or not."

"Oh, my." Christina's grandmother moved closer to the painting. "This is the creek. My goodness, the picture is so lifelike. It's like I've been transported back to that day in

May when you asked me to marry you." She smiled up at Steven, looping her arm through his.

Christina couldn't take anymore. It was as if her heart was going to beat right out of her chest.

"Grampa, Gram, we're going to head out." Luke dropped his arm from around her. "Take care Uncle Walter."

They made a hasty retreat from the house and neither she nor Luke spoke until they were safely in the car and on their way home.

"Please don't be disappointed in me," Christina said staring out of the passenger side window of Luke's Lexus RC350. The intimate interior of the luxury vehicle, with seats that felt as if they were hugging you, did nothing to comfort her. "I just wasn't ready to come clean."

"I'm not disappointed. Surprised maybe, but definitely not disappointed in you." He squeezed her thigh before returning his hand to the steering wheel. "I'm sure you'll tell them when you're ready. But…"

"But what?"

"I think it's great that your family is as close as it is, but I can't help but wonder."

"Wonder what?" She sat back in her seat feeling her defenses going up.

"If you and your family are so close, don't you think it's time you tell them who you are? You claim they're supportive and loving. Yet, you're afraid of their reaction of knowing that you're a world famous artist."

"I'm not world famous," she mumbled staring out the side window watching the city pass in a blur.

"Yet. You might not be famous yet. However with your talent, it's only a matter of time."

My cheerleader. God she loved this man.

She smiled at him even though deep down inside, she didn't feel like smiling. She felt like a wimp, unable to have a simple conversation with the people she loved most. What was wrong with her? Lately, her reasons for not sharing that part of her life didn't seem warranted, especially after seeing her grandparent's reaction to one of her paintings.

"I don't really want to be world famous," she said instead of responding to Luke's original question.

"What?" Luke stole a quick glance at her, his brows furrowed. "Are you kidding me? That's like an author saying they don't want to hit the New York Time's Bestsellers list. Those words would never come out of their mouth."

"Let me rephrase that. I wouldn't mind being famous, but I don't want people all up in my business. In our business. I want privacy. Jada has told me many stories about how fans come up to Zack for autographs or interrupt their dinners to get a photo with him. I don't want that for myself."

"No offense, but I assure you your fan base will be nothing like Zack's. He was in the public eye for years playing professional football. Big difference from being a talented artist. I'm not sure there're many people who would recognize you walking down the street even if you are their favorite artist." He reached for her hand and brought it to his lips. "But all of that is beside the point. You need to tell your family. It would be a shame for them to hear that you're Sasha Knight from someone other than you."

Yeah, that would be awful.

*

No matter how Luke dissected this *secret* of Christina's, he couldn't figure out what her real problem was in telling her family about Sasha Knight. It didn't make sense. There was a moment in her grandfather's office that Luke had been tempted to point out that Christina was the brilliant artist behind the piece, but he couldn't betray her trust like that. Even if it would've been for her own good.

He pulled onto the expressway and headed downtown. If he learned anything from spending time this afternoon with her family, it's that they loved and enjoyed each other's company. Being around them made him realize what he had missed growing up. A family. People who loved you despite your choices, good or bad. And most important, people to confide in and be there when you needed them the most. Christina had all of this and as far as he was concerned, she took it for granted.

"I need to stop by the office to pick up a file. Are you in a hurry to get home?" Luke split his attention between Christina and the road. Normally they lounged around on Sunday evenings, but he didn't want to assume she didn't have something else to do.

"No. No rush." She went back to staring out of the passenger side window.

"Listen," he grabbed hold of her hand again, "when you're ready to tell your family about Sasha Knight, you'll know. Don't let me push you into doing something you're not ready to do."

She nodded and squeezed his hand.

A while later they pulled into the parking structure connected to the rear of the law office. Luke rarely went into the office on a Sunday, but he needed to get a head start on a case he recently acquired and had failed to put the needed file in his briefcase.

"I can stay in the car and wait for you," Christina said when Luke parked.

"I don't expect to be long, but I'd feel better if you went in with me." His fingers sifted through her thick hair, pushing a few strands out of her face. Her normal bubbly attitude was missing and he hated seeing her so down on herself.

"Alright. It would be nice to see where you spend so much of your time."

They stepped into the glass-enclosed elevator that quickly took them to the twelfth floor where Atwater, Rouse & Stevenson occupied the whole level.

"Wow, this place is gorgeous," Christina said when Luke unlocked the double glass doors of the suite and signaled her in. The paintings, hanging against wallpapered walls in the receptionist area, immediately caught her attention.

"Are you familiar with the painting on the right?" Luke asked, knowing she knew her art.

"Hmm, this is one of Damien Hirst pieces. I like his style despite some critics once saying his work was amateurish and lacked finesse." She moved around the room and stopped in front of a charcoal drawing of the Scales of Justice before moving onto another painting near the receptionist's desk. "Wow, something by Georges Braque. Impressive."

Luke waited patiently while she perused the last piece of art that would lead them to the main hallway. She commented on the artist's brushwork and choice of colors as if Luke understood what she was talking about. When she was done, he draped his arm over her shoulder and escorted her down the hall.

"I'm glad you're getting a chance to see where I work. I should have invited you here long before now. So what do you think so far?"

"It's a beautiful space, but I am a little surprised that the fronts of some of the offices are glass walls. That doesn't seem very private."

"Those offices belong to the junior partners and though you can see through them, they're sound proof."

"Ahh, I see." They walked to the end of the hall. "It seems that some of you work on Sundays too," she said when they past one of Luke's associates, Attorney Arthur, who had his door open and was on the telephone. He offered a wave and they waved back.

"When I first moved to Cincinnati, I put in a few hours on Sundays. But now my baby keeps me busy doing other things." Christina grinned up at him and he placed a kiss against her temple before releasing her and unlocking his office door. He liked that he didn't have glass walls, too much of a distraction seeing people walk pass.

"Your office is as neat as your condo and bigger than my

first apartment," Christina said when she walked in. She stood in the middle of the room. "I like that despite it being large it's cozy and inviting in here. Not as intimidating as I would have imagined."

The wall-to-wall bookshelves and the woodwork in the office did give the space a warm, welcoming feel.

Christina strolled around the office taking in the small sitting area that was comprised of a sofa against the wall with two upholstered chairs facing it and a table in the center. She stopped in front of a wall that held Luke's law degree, certificates, and three plagues. At first, Luke was slow to display some of his accomplishments, not sure of how long he'd stay at the firm. Once he and Christina reunited, he had taken the time to hang up some of the items.

"Okay, now I'm impressed. You have your own bathroom." She disappeared inside, gushing about the size.

Luke stood in the doorway. The bathroom was definitely an added benefit. If the partners ever decided to move him out of the corner office, as originally planned, the bathroom would be what he would miss most.

"Maybe we can play around in here one day," Christina said in a conspiratorial whisper.

"Oh yeah. Just say when, baby." He loved the way her mind worked.

Christina shrieked when he suddenly lifted her into his arms, something he'd often done since he liked carrying her around. Instead of placing her on the bathroom counter, he took her back into his office.

"Maybe we should test out my desk before we tackle the bathroom," he said against her scented neck, turning him on more with the way she wiggled against him. He made a move to venture to the other side of her neck when he noticed some files on his desk.

"Uh, hello?" Christina frowned when he left her side. "I know that's not more important than what I *thought* we were about to do."

"I didn't leave these out," Luke said absently. He always cleared his desk and locked his drawers, as well as the office door, before leaving for the day.

Christina jumped off the desk and stood next to him. "Is that bad? Maybe your assistant laid them out for you."

"She left the office before I did Friday." He opened the top file and sifted through the first few documents, immediately recognizing notes with Gary's scribble.

Luke checked his desk drawers. Locked. He took a cursory glance around his office. His gaze scrutinized the bookshelves to the right of him and the curio cabinet across from the desk that held awards, a few binders, and a coffee machine.

Nothing looked out of place, but he didn't like people in his office, *his locked office*, when he wasn't there.

"I see you found the cases I left you," Gary Rouse said. They hadn't closed the office door completely, but that didn't give him the right to push the door all the way open. His sleazy gaze roamed the length of Christina settling a little too long on her breasts before making its way back up to her face. "I didn't expect you to start working on those cases this weekend," he said to Luke but kept his eyes on Christina. "Tomorrow is soon enough."

Luke dropped the files. His hands fisted tightly at his side and fury raged through his veins as Gary approached the desk. Christina must have sensed the tension radiating off of him. Her hand went to the center of his back, making small circles, which did nothing to tame the anger thumping inside of him.

"So, who is this beautiful woman?" Gary extended his hand, but before Christina could reach for it, Luke placed a hand on her arm, stopping her.

"My office was locked for a reason, Gary. You could have easily held on to these files until Monday."

Gary pulled his hand back and folded his arms across his chest. "I could have, but I'll be in and out tomorrow and I wanted you to get started on them first thing in the morning."

"Um, maybe I should wait out there," Christina jerked her thumb toward the door and started to move away.

"Nah, baby, you stay right here. He's the one leaving."

"Also," Gary continued as if Luke hadn't said anything, "I'll need Robin's assistance tomorrow. So hopefully you don't have plans with her. I mean for her." He returned his attention to Christina, his roving eyes doing another sweep of her body. "Have you met his assistant? Tall, redhead, green eyes? Like you, she's a looker."

"Gary, so help me," Luke said through gritted teeth, his breathing coming in short spurts. "You need to leave." The thin hold he had on the anger knotted inside him was quickly unraveling.

"Oh and since I'll be a partner soon, *you need* to get used to taking on cases you might not like. I heard about how you told Mr. Hardy that you wouldn't be taking his case. I'm not sure who you think you are, but if I give you a case, I expect…"

Something inside of Luke snapped and he lurched over the desk at Gary, knocking the telephone and files to the floor. "Your ass is—"

"Lucas no!" Christina screamed and grabbed him, her hands fisting in his shirt as she struggled to hold him back. "Please, baby. Let's just go. We need to get to that … that thing we have to do."

"Get the hell out of my office!" Luke roared, struggling against Christina's hold on him. He wanted to get his hands on Gary but didn't want to hurt Christina, who had her arms securely wrapped around him.

Gary slowly backed away, a wicked smirk on his face. "I'll go, but this conversation isn't—"

"Get out!"

Christina didn't release Luke until Gary was out of sight. She hurried across the room and locked the door.

"What is wrong with you?" She ground out as she approached Luke, her eyes shooting daggers. "I *know* you weren't about to hit that man and risk everything you've worked so hard for!"

Breathing hard, Luke leaned on his desk. With his body shaking, teeth clenched, and fury rioting inside of him, he could barely grab a hold of the control that had taken a backseat to his temper. He couldn't remember the last time someone had rattled him the way Gary seemed to enjoy doing.

Luke's heart, still beating erratically, felt as if it would leap out of his chest. He had to put a stop to this. A stop to whatever game Gary was playing.

After several deep breaths, Luke ran his hand down his face and chanced a glance at Christina. The uncertainty he saw in her eyes should have made him feel guilty about his outburst. It didn't.

"Seeing him flat on his ass with a broken jaw and a bloodied nose would have been worth the consequences."

Christina's mouth dropped open and she narrowed her eyes at him. "You're not serious! If being around that guy makes you consider doing something that stupid, you need to stay away from him. He's not worth you losing control. I could tell he was baiting you. I don't want to think about what would've happened if I weren't here."

Luke paced behind his desk, rubbing his sweaty hands down the side of his pants legs. That was the last straw. He had to do something about Gary. There was no way in hell he was going to let that asshole continue yanking his chain and pawning off his work. And the day the stupid jerk made partner, would be the day Luke quit.

Once his anger dissipated, Luke stopped pacing. Christina stood at the edge of his desk. Her wary gaze telling him that she wasn't sure what to think of him at the moment.

"I can't stand that guy. There's something about him that shoots my bullshit meter through the roof."

"I gathered as much, but Lucas you can't give him this type of control over you. Maybe you can talk to one of the senior partners about him."

Going over Gary's head was too high schoolish for Luke. No. He would handle Gary, but first he had to find out what he was up against. The guy rarely did any work, yet he was in the office most days. If he was trying to hand off his work to Luke, chances were he was doing it to someone else as well.

"Sorry about that," he mumbled.

"No need to apologize. Just promise me you won't do anything crazy and get yourself locked up."

Without making any promises, he pulled her into his arms and lowered his mouth over hers. He nipped at her lower lip, then the top one, preferring to kiss her than do any more talking. Warm. Soft. Delicious. Her sweet kisses were all he needed as desire quickly squashed the battle that was brewing inside of him. If only he could keep her by his side 24/7 to surround him with the peace that only she could provide, the better he would be.

Reluctantly, Luke broke off the kiss. Touching his forehead to hers he said, "I hate that you had to witness … all of that."

"Me too. I know you're going to do whatever you want to do, but be careful. Okay?"

He gave a slight nod. "Why don't we save our office rendezvous for another time. 'Cause right now I want to get you home and horizontal so that I can make love to you as promised earlier."

A slow smile spread across her mouth and she batted those big beautiful eyes at him. "Well then, don't just stand there. Let's go."

Luke chuckled. Forgetting about Gary, he grabbed the file he had originally come in for and gave thanks for the beautiful angel who had dropped into his life. Tonight he planned to expend all of his pent up energy on pleasing her, but tomorrow, he was going to figure out what to do about Gary. The man was going to regret getting in his face.

CHAPTER TEN

Christina yawned for what seemed like the hundredth time doing everything she could to stay awake. It was already ten o'clock at night and she couldn't leave the art studio until she finished the painting she was working on. The last piece needed for her show in Chicago in three weeks.

She set down her brush and scooted her stool back, cringing when the metal legs scraped against the concrete floor. The floors weren't painted, but she didn't want to do any more damage than was already done to them. For two years now, she rented the one room space that had an attached bathroom and a small kitchen area. The room was nothing to brag about, but it beat having to paint at the loft. Most importantly, she liked not having the models in her home. They were wonderful to work with, but she definitely wanted to keep her personal life separate from her business.

Standing, Christina lifted her arms high above her head, reached as far up as she could and stretched. "Alright, Luke, where are you?" She dropped her arms and shook them out. A quick glance at the clock on the far wall revealed that he was late. He had called an hour earlier, agreeing to bring her dinner once he left the office, and she was beyond hungry.

She tidied her workspace, placing brushes she wouldn't be using for the rest of the night into a can of paint thinner. A couple of more hours and she should be able to call it a night. All she had to do was figure out how to stay awake.

Checking her cell to make sure she hadn't missed a call, she thought about Luke's encounter with that slimeball attorney. She could only hope he was telling the truth when he said there hadn't been any other altercations. This week he hadn't talked much about work, seeming a bit more distracted than usual.

"Come on, Luke." She needed to get back to work, but couldn't focus when her stomach was growling.

Feeling a little restless, she strolled over to her iPod speaker and cranked up the volume. When working on nudes, she usually painted to the tunes of Tupac or R. Kelly. The raunchier the lyrics, the better.

She shuffled through her playlist and stopped when she found the album she'd been searching for.

"Oh yeah." Nothing got her creative juices flowing like music.

Catching the beat, Christina snapped her fingers. She bobbed her head and rocked her hips as R. Kelly's song "Leg's Shakin'", pumped through the speakers. Wiggling back over to her painting, she twirled and dipped just as the door buzzer rang.

Even after months together, a sweet thrill of excitement soared through her veins whenever Luke showed up. She hurried to the intercom near the door.

"Who is it?" she asked and released the intercom button.

"It's me." She buzzed him up.

The moment she heard footsteps, she swung open the door. Luke was barely in front of the entrance before she leaped into his arms and wrapped her legs around his waist.

"Whoa, baby!" He chuckled and bumped into the doorjamb as he held her tight with one arm around her waist, his other hand holding a bag with their dinner.

Christina squealed when he bent forward, thinking he was going to drop her. Instead, he released the bag he was holding and held her with both arms.

"Are you happy to see me?" He covered her mouth before she could respond, her lips parting automatically. Luke closed the door with his foot and backed her to a wall. Christina moaned as their tongues tangled. His kiss as potent as usual. "Mmm, I'll take that as a yes." He gave her one last kiss before slowly lowering her to the floor.

"I'm *very* happy to see you." She kissed him on the cheek and hurried to the bag he left at the door. "Unbelievably happy."

"Yeah right." He stuffed his hand in the front pocket of his jeans. "I have a feeling you're more excited about seeing that food than you are me."

"Never." She walked around him and over to her art table carrying the bag. Once she pushed paints and her brushes out of the way, she pulled out a salad, two soft bread sticks, and utensils. "Hmm …I wish you would have brought fried chicken."

Luke's brows drew together. "Since when did you start eating meat?"

"I haven't. I just wish you would have brought some." She'd been a vegetarian for almost nine months now and it was a struggle. For as long as she could remember, she'd had a healthy appetite and it seemed lately she couldn't get full.

"Well, if you want chicken, I'll go and find you some. Or whatever else you want."

"Nah, that's okay. I just had a moment." The last thing she needed was to give Martina and the others an opportunity to talk about her not following through with her vegetarian diet. She unwrapped the utensils and dug into her salad. "Where's yours?" she asked between bites.

"I ate earlier." He stood in front of her easel studying her latest piece, his hands still in his pockets. "Is your music loud enough?"

"Not really. I wanted to make sure I heard the buzzer when you arrived."

He grinned and shook his head.

Christina let her gaze wander down his body. She could look at him all day. She loved seeing him in a suit, but no man could rock a pair of jeans the way her man could. The pair he had on emphasized his long legs and thick thighs. Zoning in on his perfect butt, something stirred within her.

"What do you think?" she asked when he turned from the painting and headed to the upholstered chair in a nearby corner of the room. She was almost done with the painting but needed to do some blending of color in the background.

"I think it's amazing, as usual."

Maybe she was more insecure about her work than she thought because heat rose to her cheeks at his compliment.

"Not many artists can be talented in different art styles, but you have nailed three of them –landscapes, abstract, and nudes. I'm beyond impressed." He stretched his long legs out in front of him and crossed them at the ankle. Laying his head on the back of the chair, he looked more tired than she felt. "What do you think about when you're sketching or painting a male model?"

She stuffed a fork full of salad into her mouth and turned slightly to better see her painting. He hadn't asked many questions regarding her models, male or female and she was a little surprised he hadn't asked about them sooner.

"I think about you."

His left eyebrow rose a fraction. "Is that right?" His voice dropped an octave, into a sexy vibe. With the way, he watched her, and R. Kelly crooning erotic lyrics in the background, she suddenly wasn't as hungry. At least not for food.

"When you're positioning your models, for just the right pose, what's going through your mind?

"Thoughts of you. I envision *you* posing. I think about the angles I want to capture and the feelings I want to evoke through the painting, but always, my mind is filled with thoughts of you."

It was suddenly getting a little warm in the room. All their talk about models and posing had her body humming.

She set her salad on the art table, not taking her eyes from Luke, who watched her intently. Her pounding heart kicked up a notch. So much for the air conditioner. Luke only had to look at her and she got all hot and bothered.

"I'm starting to see a pattern in your responses."

She stood and unhooked the straps of her paint-splattered coveralls. She let the front bib fall to her waist, giving a better view of the blue tube topped she wore underneath. She almost smiled when she heard his intake of breath. The thin shirt made it obvious that she was braless.

"That's because when I'm drawing or painting nudes, I think of you," she said seductively.

He slouched down in his seat, one of his hands rubbing the short stubble on his chin. "I see."

What she saw was desire swimming in his eyes. He might've been trying to play it cool, but no doubt he felt what she felt. Heat. Desire. And the need to get naked.

"I hear you rockin' some of R. Kelly's tunes. How do you decide what music to listen to while you're painting?"

"Depends on how I'm feeling."

"And how are you feeling?"

"Prurient. Libidinous. Horny as hell."

Luke cleared his throat and chuckled. "I see."

Christina laughed. "I see? Heck, for a person who has such an extensive vocabulary, you sure aren't showing it off tonight."

She grabbed the upright chair that was near the art table and pulled it to the center of the floor. After working nonstop for the past four hours, it was time she took a proper break and have a little fun in the process.

She turned back to Luke. He was so damn cocky, but

tonight she planned to bring the brother to his knees.

Her fingers teased the bottom of her tube top as she swayed her hips to the beat, becoming one with the rhythm of the music. The pleasure that came with being with a man you loved, a man who adored you was one of the most satisfying feelings she had ever experienced.

Still rocking to the tunes, Christina took her time and lifted the thin material of her shirt. Inch, by inch, by salacious inch. No matter how in control he was trying to be, she knew it was only a matter of time, when the sight of her bare breasts would short-circuit his brain. No doubt he was almost at that point. The perspiration gracing his hairline a tell-tale sign that she was turning him on as much as she was turning herself on.

He scooted lower in his chair and adjusted himself. Oh yeah, she definitely had his attention.

She pulled the top over her head and tossed the material to the floor, her breast hanging free as she gyrated to the music. Luke sat staring. No, actually it was more like gawking. Gone was that confident air that he wore like a shield, and in its place was the look of desire.

Christina loved to strip for him, loving how he responded.

She crooked her index finger back and forth, giving him her most seductive smile, and summoned him over to the chair, her gaze holding his. For a moment, she thought he would continue sitting there, staring, no words or reaction, but then he sat upright in his seat.

A burst of giddiness shot through her as Luke toed off his shoes. It was only a matter of time before they came together.

Standing slowly, he flashed that crooked, sexy grin that always made her wet. Her heart hammered wildly when he lifted his T-shirt over his head, his muscular chest and flat abs on full display. The man had a body that was meant to be caressed, licked and worshiped. And she planned to do all of the above.

She bit down lightly on her bottom lip and watched as he took his time walking toward her. Her heart rate picked up in speed. Luke slowed his steps, unbuckled his belt, and carefully unzipped his jeans.

Christina was cool. Staying in control, at least until he stopped. He snaked his tongue across his lower lip and cupped his package.

Damn him!

He hadn't even stepped out of his pants and she was already panting and squeezing her thighs together. Knowing that he had her complete attention, he let his pants drop around his ankles and stood in the middle of the floor, his erection pressing firmly against his black boxer briefs. Suddenly she wasn't the one controlling this show. As a matter of fact, she was about ready to scream uncle and pounce on his ass.

She was enraptured by the slow, precise movement of his hand, stroking himself. She found the way he gripped and massaged his package, sexy as hell. The throbbing between her legs grew more intense and she teetered on the edge of control.

Luke finally claimed the chair that she had placed in the center of the floor, still holding and caressing himself, watching her behind lower lids. "Don't let me interrupt your little show," he said.

Yes, this had been her show, but somehow, within minutes, he had distracted her with his erotic moves. But there was a chance that she could regain some of the control.

Suddenly the song in the background changed and R. Kelly started singing about licking Oreos and giving up the cookie.

How appropriate.

Christina fiddled with the two buttons on each side of the coveralls, her gaze locked with Luke's as he sang along with one of his favorite music artist. Christina undid the buttons and let the material slide down her legs.

Luke sat up and she almost burst out laughing when his mouth dropped open.

"Damn, girl."

He acted as if he had never seen her naked before. He was out of his briefs and had sheathed himself faster than she had ever seen him move before.

"Have I ever told you that I'm glad you're not a fan of underwear?"

She cleared her throat, distracted by his thick shaft. "You might have mentioned it a time or two."

Something inside her stirred. The lustful glint in his eyes practically forced her to move. *Really* feeling the music, she snapped her fingers above her head and bounced to the beat as she eased up on him.

Luke groaned. "Aw, baby. You're killing me here." His arm snaked out and pulled her to him. He lowered his head to her breast and flicked his silky tongue around her hardened nipple before pulling the taut bud into his mouth.

Christina whimpered as he stroked, teased, sucked. With each lash of his tongue, heat singed every nerve ending within her and she gripped his upper arms to keep from sliding to the floor. He performed the same pleasures on her other breast, the sweet torture almost too much.

"This seduction scene has been fun, but I need to be inside you," Luke said in a husky groan when he made his way back up to her lips. He ran his hands down her hips and palmed her butt, moving rhythmically in beat to the music, his mouth ravishing hers. Christina felt as if she would burst if he weren't inside of her soon.

As if Luke were reading her mind, he lifted his head and backed them up to the chair. She straddled his lap and cried out with pleasure when he entered her in one smooth motion.

"Ah, yeah," she moaned, her eyes closed and her body slowly adjusting to his size. She savored the feel of him inside of her, rotating her hips wanting, needing to feel all of him. The wood chair creaked under their weight, but Christina was too far gone to care whether it held them or not.

Luke's large hands gripped the bottom of her thighs, lifting her up and down his slick shaft. Christina held on for the ride as he went faster, harder, deeper. Her sensitive nipples grazed his chest with every move, sending a whole new wave of pleasure pulsing through her body.

"Luke," she said on a breath, unable to form any other words, barely able to breathe.

He picked up speed, thumping in and out of her like a man possessed and she loved every moment. She loved the intensity she saw wading in his eyes. She loved the erotic sounds he made as he plunged even deeper.

A surge of ecstasy throbbed through Christina's body and her stomach tighten. Heat sizzled along her spine and her body bucked and bounced on top of Luke. She was losing her grip on her control, her climax within reach. One powerful thrust and Christina screamed out, her nails digging into Luke's shoulders as she surrendered to the whirl of sensation that hurled her over the edge.

Luke growled his release with such force, his fingers digging into the skin of her thighs as the turbulence of his explosion rocked them both. Christina's heavy breathing mingled with his and they collapsed against each other.

"Maybe we can just stay like this," she wheezed, her head resting in the crook of his neck. "I don't think I can move."

"Fine by me," he panted near her ear, "you done wore me out."

Christina had no idea of how long they sat there. Her limbs were weak, her mind blank.

"That was intense." Luke held her tighter keeping her in place, his breathing almost back to normal. When she lifted her head from his shoulder, her hair covered her face and Luke brushed it back with his hands. Of course, there were a few stubborn strands that wouldn't cooperate. After several tries, he finally had the wayward curls under control, holding them back while he cupped her face between his hands, forcing her to look at him. "Can we agree that you won't listen to anything by R. Kelly unless I'm here? I wouldn't want any of your models to reap anything remotely close to what you just gave me."

A smile tilted her lips. She loved how understanding he'd been. Most men would feel insecure and probably act a fool knowing their woman had naked men posing for her for hours sometimes.

She nodded and placed a kiss on his lips. "I think that's definitely something I can agree to. Besides, nobody else turns me on the way you do. Not even when R. Kelly is singing in the background."

CHAPTER ELEVEN

Christina didn't care how many art shows she participated in, her gut twisted with anxiety every time. The Chicago show was no different. Despite Luke's presence, insecurity wrapped around her like an unwanted cold, refusing to give her any peace and she couldn't seem to shake the anxious unease.

She and Luke had arrived in town three hours earlier, their visit starting out perfect. They checked into the hotel, and it hadn't taken long for them to strip down and take advantage of the luxury accommodations, specifically the king sized bed. Christina didn't think she would ever get enough of Luke. Even after months of being back together, it was as if they were still trying to make up for lost time. Still getting reacquainted with each other's body.

Christina moved slowly around the open space, her heels clicking against the shiny hardwood floor. The gallery was hosting three other artists, whose styles varied considerably, giving her a chance to check out the other talent.

She stopped in front of a piece entitled: Between the Tides. Perusing the dramatic oil painting, rich with blues, gold and purples she immediately felt as if she was looking down from heaven viewing a cyclone hovering above the earth. *Outstanding.* The colors complimented each other and the artist's brush techniques were precise.

She continued on her tour of other paintings, glancing over her shoulder once to see if Luke had returned. He had reluctantly stepped outside a moment ago to take a telephone call from his office.

Christina slowed again when she reached an abstract painting, appreciating the artist's unique way of using a combination of techniques. She always preferred shows where she wasn't the only artist featured. Less pressure. Less stress. She had four nude pieces and two abstracts on display. Already she noticed two of her paintings had *sold* signs hanging from them. This was her fifth show in two years and so far they all had been successful with her selling all of her paintings either during the show or shortly after.

"Sorry it took me so long," Luke said when he came up behind her, placing a kiss near her right ear. "I thought I had taken care of everything at work before we left this morning, but sure enough, an issue popped up that I hadn't anticipated."

Christina turned to face him as he stuffed his cell phone into the inside pocket of his suit jacket. Tonight he hadn't worn a tie and instead left the top three buttons of his striped dress shirt undone, a gold curb chain hanging around his neck. That bad boy persona he rocked so effortlessly was in full effect, turning her on without him even trying. He looked sexier than usual and more relaxed. His workload had practically doubled in the last two months, but according to him, he still wasn't putting in the type of hours he had while in New York.

"No problem. I'm glad you were able to come with me. I can't tell you how good it feels to share one of my shows with someone. Jada attended my first one, but normally it's just me standing around trying to blend in."

"What are you talking about? I attended your last show

with you."

"That was different. You didn't know that I was Sasha Knight at the time."

He nodded. "True. Now some things I noticed back then make sense, like why you seemed to be on edge that night. I had also noticed you checking out the people in attendance, more so than the art displayed."

"Yeah. That was a stressful weekend. Between knowing I couldn't travel with you that next day and displaying the nudes for the first time, I'm glad I didn't have a heart attack. Talk about stress." She shook her head thinking about that night. She had no way of knowing how her paintings would go over. Everyone wasn't comfortable viewing nudes, but that had ended up being one of her most successful shows.

"Well, I'm glad that weekend is behind us though I still wish you would have told me what was going on. It would have relieved you of a lot of unnecessary anxiety."

"I know. That will be the last time I keep something from you."

She stepped closer and slid her hands slowly up his chest, needing to be near him, feel him.

"You know if you keep touching me like this, I'm going to pull you into the nearest broom closet and have my way with you." He snaked his arm around her waist and nuzzled her neck. Having her hair piled up on top of her head also gave him easy access to place feathery kisses against the sensitive spot behind her ear.

"I like the way you think. Maybe we—"

"There you are. I was hoping you hadn't snuck out yet," Christina's agent said. Valerie Cook was a ball of energy and talked a mile per minute. Christina didn't know if she was on a natural high, or if her high came from the four cups of black coffee she consumed on a daily basis. "There are some important people in attendance who are very interested in your work."

"Valerie, we already talked about this. I know you think I

should reveal myself as the artist, but I'm not interested. I don't want the attention. I prefer staying anonymous."

"CJ," she said on a frustrated sigh and turned to Luke. "Can't you talk your girlfriend into stepping into the spotlight? She would sell twice as many pieces and I'm sure there are a number of buyers who would love to commission her work. Look at her." She grabbed Christina's chin. "She's absolutely gorgeous. This face alone would get her a ton of business. Add her talent and how fast she paints and she'd be a millionaire by the end of the year."

Luke pulled Christina closer, forcing Valerie to drop her hand. Christina had already told him about her overzealous agent, and how she was trying to get Christina to reveal herself as Sasha Knight.

"I agree Valerie. She is stunning. But I think we should respect her decision. Her talent alone is enough to sell out at every show."

"Ugh, you two," Valerie said exasperated. She had to be the most dramatic person Christina had ever met. Instead of being an art agent, she should really consider a career in acting. Surely Christina wasn't the only artist who preferred to hide behind a pseudonym. "Fine. We'll keep doing it your way." Spotting someone she knew, her agent waltzed across the room in her usual exuberant fashion.

"Damn she's a piece of work."

"You have no idea." Christina stepped out of his arms and smoothed down the front of her blouse as she glanced around the space. The beautiful gallery had a bronze color fabric draping a portion of the ceiling dramatically, with the ends falling midway down some of the exposed brick walls. There were twice as many people in attendance than when they first arrived. "Valerie is really starting to get on my nerves with her persistence," Christina said when she noticed her agent fluttering around a small group of people standing near one of Christina's paintings. "I'm not sure what the big deal is, but she's been calling me every couple of weeks trying to get me to change my mind."

"Yeah, she does come across as having another motive besides selling more paintings. Do you still need her? Are you able to set up showings on your own now?"

"I probably could, but it's not something I want to take on. Between working during the day and painting at night and on the weekends, there's not much time for anything else."

Luke continued watching Valerie. When he first met her, he had made a comment about her being a bit shady. He didn't like that she couldn't look him in the eye and she talked a mile a minute, seeming to glaze over important information. Christina assumed she was just a little high strung. Okay maybe very high strung, but harmless.

For the next thirty minutes, they roamed around the gallery's second level and Christina felt truly blessed. In the big scheme of things, she considered herself a newbie, especially compared to some of the other artists whose work was on display. Yet, some of her pieces had already sold and there was still one more day left.

Feeling the hairs on the back of her neck rise, Christina stopped and glanced around. Luke had stepped outside again to take a call and from the moment he walked away, she felt as if she were being watched.

She stood next to a wrought-iron railing, her gaze taking in her surroundings. Maybe she was overreacting. No one stood out.

Shaking her head at her skittish behavior, she headed back downstairs hoping to run into Luke.

Okay, something is definitely off. And that's when she spotted him. A man dressed in all black openly stared at her. Unease crept up her spine and a shiver shot through her body.

Looking away, Christina rubbed her hands up and down her bare arms to eliminate the goose bumps. She had noticed him earlier, and didn't think much of it, but now …

She turned and headed toward the front entrance. Hopefully, Luke wouldn't be on his call too much longer.

Finding a spot off to the side of the main door, she turned back and glanced in the direction she had just come from. Sure enough, the man's steely gaze was still locked on her. He nodded, but Christina diverted her gaze, not wanting to encourage any interaction.

She startled when someone placed a hand on her shoulder and jerked around barely holding back a scream. "Luke, oh my God, you scared me to death. I didn't see you come back in."

*

Luke's eyes narrowed at Christina's reaction, her eyes round with fear. His protective instinct immediately kicked in.

"What's going on?" He placed a hand at the back of her neck and gently pulled her close. "You okay?" His lips gently touched hers as he caressed her cheeks. Christina wasn't the jumpy type. Something had spooked her.

"I'm fine, but there's this guy over my left shoulder who keeps staring at me, the man with a camera hanging around his neck."

Luke discreetly glanced over her shoulder and sure enough, there was an older man looking directly at them. Average height with a café au lait complexion, he wore a black beret and wire rim glasses. He didn't look familiar.

Keeping his gaze on the man and hoping to calm Christina, Luke said, "You're a very beautiful woman. Of course, he would stare. Are you sure you don't know him?"

"Positive."

Luke didn't know who the guy was, but he had every intention of finding out.

When the man in question headed in their direction, Luke stepped in front of Christina, partially blocking her.

"Excuse me, can I get a picture?" he directed the question to Christina.

"No, you can't get a picture. Who are you?" Luke kept his voice low, but couldn't keep the venom from his tone. Who walked up to people at an art gallery asking to get a picture of a perfect stranger?

"I'm with The Artist in Us magazine. I heard that your companion is Sasha Knight.

Shit.

"And where did you hear that?"

"From a reliable source." The man fidgeted under Luke's scrutiny, sending off signals that he was lying.

Christina stiffened next to Luke and before either of them could respond, the man snapped several pictures.

"What the hell!" Luke growled. He reached out and placed his hand over the long lens, yanking the camera out of the man's grip.

"Hey!" The guy attempted to grab the camera, but Luke shot him a scathing look, daring him to come any closer. "Give that back to me!"

"Not until I erase the photos." Luke pushed a few buttons until he found the right one that would delete the pictures of Christina. He shoved the man's camera back at him. "If we see any photos of her anywhere or if you ever approach her again, you *and* that magazine better find a damn good lawyer."

With his cell phone, Luke snapped a few pictures of the man and then grabbed Christina by the hand. "Let's go."

CHAPTER TWELVE

Weeks later and Christina was still thinking about her show in Chicago. Despite the night ending with the pushy photographer who had invaded her space, all of her paintings had sold. Sasha Knight would soon be a household name when it came to art. Some days she couldn't believe her success. Everything seemed to happen so fast when in reality this is what she had been working toward since high school.

She wasn't the only one who was excited about her success. Her agent, Valerie, was beside herself, eager for Christina to create more *masterpieces*. She had called earlier to let Christina know that the Chicago gallery was interested in hosting another show for her in six months. Christina couldn't ask for better news, but she hadn't been painting as much, which meant she didn't have many pieces. And the man with the camera that night in Chicago made her realize just how much she hated being in the public's eye.

Christina pulled the tossed salad she had made earlier out of the refrigerator and set it on the counter next to the bottle of wine. Friday nights, when Luke wasn't working late, had become their movie night as well as her favorite night of the week.

A soft knock sounded. *Ahh, think about him and he shall appear.*

Christina opened the door smiling. "Hey there."

"Hey, yourself." Luke walked in and set the pizza box and movies on the counter. He gathered her in his arms and lifted her in the air.

"Oh my God! What are you doing?" She squealed, giggling uncontrollably when he spun her around. "Put me down. What's gotten into you?"

"You, baby." He set her on her feet and kissed her. This, all of it, was what Christina looked forward to at the end of a busy workweek. Him, a night at home, and pizza – even if it was a vegetable pizza.

With a hand at the back of his head, Christina held him close, desiring to put everything she had into the kiss. He tasted like peppermint with just a hint of nicotine. She loved him dearly, but she had to convince him, once and for all, to give up the smokes.

With one last peck on his lips, she leaned her head back to look at him.

"You have to quit smoking. And before you try to deny anything, I can taste the evidence."

"What if I can't quit?" He rested his forehead against hers.

"Then we can't kiss."

He dropped his arms from around her waist and stepped back. "So, are you saying that if I don't quit we're through?"

Christina recognized the defensiveness in his tone, but it didn't scare her. Instead, it showed her just how accustomed he was to losing people and she knew he was afraid of losing her ... again.

"I'm *never* walking away from you," she said with conviction watching him closely. "You're stuck with me whether you quit smoking or not."

His grin was slow in coming, but his eyes brimmed with love. "Really?" He reached for her again and lowered his mouth over hers, but she placed a finger against his lips, stopping him within an inch of meeting her mouth.

"I said you would never lose me. I never said anything about you being able to kiss me again."

He hesitated, but then laughed. "There is no way I can be near you and not kiss you."

"Well?"

"Well, I guess the cigarettes have to go."

Christina narrowed her eyes and folded her arms. "Don't say you're going to do something until you know you can do it."

"Baby, if it means having free access to that luscious mouth of yours, the last cigarette I had will be the last one I have." He pecked her on the lips. "Now, let's eat and get this movie started before you fall asleep."

"Me? You're the one who can't seem to stay awake past the first five minutes of a movie unless you're eating."

"That's because the last three or four movies you picked were girly and I don't do chick flicks."

"You don't even give them a chance."

"Well, you don't have to worry about me falling asleep on the ones we're watching tonight. Between Denzel Washington and Samuel L. Jackson, I'll probably be able to pull an all-nighter."

Christina rolled her eyes. "Yeah we'll see. If you grab the pizza and the wine, I can carry everything else."

Christina had turned her third bedroom into a small den with a pullout couch, walnut coffee tables, and colorful floor pillows strategically placed around the room. The fifty-inch flat screen television was a gift from Luke. Apparently, thirty-six inches wasn't big enough for optimal basketball watching.

Once they were settled, Luke picked up the remote for the DVD player.

"Before you start the movie, I made a decision today," Christina said.

Luke turned toward her, his arm behind her on the back of the sofa. "And what's that?"

"This Sunday I'm going to tell my parents and grandparents about Sasha Knight. It's way past time, especially with that guy in Chicago taking pictures. I know you deleted them from his camera, but who knows if he has others. I don't want my family to find out like that."

Luke nodded. "I think you're doing the right thing and I have no doubt they're going to support you. And even if there are some doubters in the bunch, I'll always be here rallying behind you in whatever you decide to do."

Christina couldn't stop the smile from spreading across her face. Considering a large part of Luke's life was spent with him looking out and supporting himself, he had a great handle on what it meant to be there for someone else. What it meant to be a family.

"So does your decision mean that you're going to officially let the world know who you are?" He massaged the back of her neck, his touch sending tingles through her body. If he kept it up, there might be another reason why they wouldn't make it through the movies.

"No. I'm still going to paint as Sasha Knight, but I want to continue to maintain a low profile. After that conversation that you and I had on our way back from Chicago, about my work becoming more popular, I don't think I'm cut out to do shows. I'm uncomfortable watching people peruse my artwork and I definitely don't like the idea of people taking pictures of me. More than that, I don't want my face in newspapers or magazines. I like things just the way they are."

"Hold up. You're not planning to do any more shows?"

"If I do a show it might only be one a year and I doubt if I'll attend." She placed a slice of pizza on a paper plate and handed it to Luke before getting a slice for herself. "I'll be meeting with my agent in a couple of weeks to discuss a few things, but I'm open to doing some commissioned work and maybe just sell a few pieces online."

"Okay, I'm going to say this, but it's not that I'm trying to control you or anything like that. As for the commissioned projects, I'm not comfortable with the idea of you doing nudes. Too many crazy people out here and I don't want you to end up in any compromising situations."

Christina nodded. "I agree. My commission work will only include abstract or landscapes. As far as the nudes, I think I might give that up. Not sure yet."

"Well, whatever you decide, I'm here for you," he said in his Barry White voice.

Christina grinned and shook her head, hoping he wasn't going to sing. Instead, he loaded their paper plates with food and turned on the movie. But before she could take a bite, the doorbell rang.

"Are you expecting someone?" Luke paused the movie.

"Nope."

Christina went to the intercom mounted on the wall near the door. She pressed the button that would allow her to see visitors without them being able to see her. When the person came into view, she gasped and her hand flew to her chest.

"What's he doing here?"

Luke peered over her shoulder. "Only one way to find out." When Christina didn't make a move to talk to her grandfather through the intercom, Luke did the honors. He gave him instructions on how to reach the top floor and then buzzed him in.

"He knows." Christina paced in front of the door. "I can't believe he knows."

Luke grabbed her by the shoulders, stopping her in her tracks. "You don't know that. Let's find out what's going on before you get yourself all worked up."

Christina appreciated Luke trying to keep her from jumping to conclusions, but there was no other reason her grandfather would show up especially without calling. He rarely went anywhere at night unless he and her grandmother were attending an event.

Christina pulled in a deep breath and opened the door just as Steven Jenkins stepped off the elevator.

"Pretty fancy setup you have here," her grandfather said and kissed Christina on the cheek. "But you really should get one of the guys at the shop to see about updating that elevator. That deathtrap is an accident waiting to happen. How are you, Luke?"

Luke smirked at Christina, no doubt enjoying the fact that her grandfather had pretty much second what he'd been saying all along about the elevator. He shook Steven's extended hand.

"I'm doing well, sir. It's good to see you again."

"Grampa, what are you doing here? I thought we all agreed that you shouldn't be driving around at night." His eyesight wasn't as good as it used to be and her uncles had insisted that he get a driver or have one of them take him where he needed to go.

"Just because the family thought that was a good idea doesn't mean I agreed," he said gruffly, walking farther into the room.

"Grampa." Christina's hands were on her hips and she narrowed her eyes giving him a similar look that her grandmother used on him. "You know the family is right."

"Do you see what I have to go through?" Steven asked Luke.

"Yes. I know the feeling."

"I'm sure you do." Her grandfather returned his attention to Christina. "If it makes you feel any better, I have a driver who brought me over here. He's out in the car, but my eyesight is fine. It's so good that I was able to read this." He handed Christina The Artist in Us magazine and her heart dropped even before seeing her photo plastered on the page.

Oh no.

She skimmed the article, which mentioned her and her work that was on display recently in Chicago. Interestingly enough, she realized that the picture couldn't have been taken that weekend. She'd had on all black both days. In this particular photo, she had on the red sweater dress she wore in New York.

She glanced up to find her grandfather staring at her. "I can explain."

"Please do. I'm wondering how it is that one of my granddaughters is a world famous artist and I didn't know about it."

Luke stepped forward, his hand at the small of her back. "I'll be in the family room if you need me, but I think it's time you two had a talk," he spoke the words to her, but they were loud enough for her grandfather to hear. Kissing Christina on the cheek, he gave her grandfather a nod and then disappeared down the hall.

Christina already knew it was well past time for her to tell her grandfather about her other life. What had started as her fun little secret, a hobby that helped relieve stress, an outlet to express herself, had turned into so much more. Another career, but lately a thorn in her side with all of the secrecy.

She and her grandfather sat on the sofa and she marveled at how good he still looked. They had recently celebrated his seventy-seventh birthday. With his imposing size and head full of hair and no wrinkles, he could easily pass for a man who was twenty years younger.

"You must have gone to great lengths to keep this a secret. Apparently, you kept it from your cousin Jada too because she hasn't said a word. And we both know she can't keep anything to herself."

Christina burst out laughing at that. Jada and her inability to keep a secret was one of the running jokes in the family. Normally if anyone told her cousin something was a secret, it didn't take five minutes for her to find someone to tell.

"Believe it or not, she's known since the beginning and I honestly thought she would have blabbed it by now."

"Miracles never cease," her grandfather mumbled and sat back on the sofa, his long legs stretched out in front of him. He was one of the most patient men she has ever known and she knew he would sit there all night if need be for her to start talking.

"I never intended for my art to take off the way it has and once it did," she shrugged, "I wanted to keep the success to myself."

Her grandfather's brows drew together. "Why? I'm sure the family would have loved to cheer you on and support this endeavor. I know I would have, had I known. I don't understand why you felt you had to keep secrets."

At this moment, her extreme actions did seem a bit childish.

"I had a couple of reasons. One, I didn't want any negative vibes interrupting my creative flow. All it would have taken was for someone in the family to tell me that I was wasting my time. Or if someone had criticized my work, I might have put down my brushes. Also, doing art on the side, when you expect me to work and support the family business, it felt a little disloyal. I guess I didn't want to let you or the rest of the family down."

"CJ, I have always taught you kids that family comes first, but I never meant for you to put your dreams on hold. I don't want you to ever feel as if you have to pick working at the family business over pursuing your career. Your family will always be here for you, *always* no matter what you do … or what you paint.

Heat crept up her cheeks, and Christina thought she would die right then and there. What if he knew about the nude paintings? A quick glance at him, his eyebrow raised with a knowing look in his eyes, and she was pretty sure he knew.

That's just great.

She cleared her throat. "Thanks, Grampa. I'm sorry I kept this from you, but I just didn't want it to be like it was for dad."

Her grandfather tilted his head and frowned. "How what was for your dad?"

"I heard that when he talked about playing the drums professionally, Uncle Carlton and Uncle Ben told him not to quit his day job. They said he would never be able to play the drums or the sax professionally, that he wasn't good enough."

Her grandfather chuckled. "I can't say that I remember any of that, but it's probably true. Honey, how often have Peyton, Jerry or even Martina picked on you about one thing or another?"

"More times than I can count." She thought back on the night the girls helped her unpack boxes.

"That's because that's what family does. You know that. They say things to you or about you that others can't get away with. It doesn't mean they don't love you or aren't willing to support and encourage you. As far as I'm concern, it's your family who helps give you a thick skin, able to handle criticism from anyone who is not kin. And as for your father, his musical skills are nothing like your abilities with paint and a canvas."

All Christina could do was shake her head. All this time she fretted over nothing. Of course some of her family would give her a hard time, but she knew that the love in the Jenkins family ran deep. Even if she were to embarrass them with some of her work, they wouldn't love her any less.

"And another thing, your father was never as serious about music as you seem to be about painting. Have you ever asked him about that time in his life?"

"It's come up here and there, but he never seemed to be all that interested in discussing his music. I assumed it was a sore subject."

"Talk to him. I think you'll be surprised to know that for your dad, playing the drums or the sax was more of a hobby than anything else."

Hours later, Christina and Luke lay in bed talking. "How do you feel now that your grandfather knows about Sasha Knight?"

"Like an anvil has been lifted off of my chest." She laughed. "I can't believe I didn't give him or the family more credit. Granted everyone doesn't know yet, but I'm sure once they find out, some will be supportive while others will tease me. MJ is going to have a field day regarding the nudes."

Christina wished she would have made better decisions regarding Sasha Knight long before now. She almost lost the only man she'd ever loved, and she kept an unnecessary secret from the people who would always love her. She still planned to tell everyone Sunday.

"I'm thinking we should celebrate this new found freedom you're feeling now that everything is out in the open."

"What do you have in mind?"

Luke turned off the bedside table lamp and gathered her in his arms. "I can show you better than I can tell you."

CHAPTER THIRTEEN

"I'm telling you he's expecting me."

Christina rolled her eyes, barely keeping her temper in check. How many times did she have to keep repeating herself? If she weren't so hungry, she'd smash the bag of food she was carrying with her and Luke's lunch, into his assistant's face. She couldn't. She had been looking forward to the vegetable lasagna from her favorite Italian restaurant all day, and there was no way she would waste it on this woman.

I should have brought in my cell phone.

The woman stood behind her desk and looked Christina up and down, her eyes narrowed and her ruby red lips cocked in a frown. Just because Christina had worn her painter whites didn't give this woman the right to look at her as if she smelled something bad. Her clothes were clean and didn't have a lick of paint on them, yet the redhead was judging her.

That Sunday in Luke's office, Gary was right. Robin was a looker. Long red hair, startling green eyes, and her pouty lips probably got her plenty of dates, if she weren't married. Christina hoped she was married. *Please be married.* The thought of this woman working so closely with Luke made her little green-eyed monster show its wicked head. Luke had never given her a reason not to trust him, but she wouldn't put anything past this spitfire of a woman, who could easily grace the cover of any fashion magazine.

"Who did you say you were again?" Robin asked.

"Christina Jenkins." Her voice sounded calmer than she felt. With only an hour for lunch, Christina didn't have time for this nonsense. And where was Luke anyway? He knew she was joining him for lunch at noon, and it was ten after. He should have been waiting in the receptionist area for her.

"Hmm, you're not on his schedule."

"That doesn't mean he's not expecting me. Call him."

"I'm sorry Ms. Jenkins, but he's with a client, and he has back to back meetings this afternoon. Would you like to leave a message for him?"

"No. I'll wait."

"I don't think that's a good—"

"I'll wait."

"Fine. You can have a seat over there." Robin pointed to a set of chairs about ten feet away.

"I'll stand."

"Suit yourself," the woman murmured.

Christina turned and glanced around the space. She was definitely under dressed. The majority of the people were men, but there were a few women moving about who looked as if they were participating in a fashion show.

Humph. I'll take my painter whites any day.

While waiting, Christina roamed to the receptionist area not wanting to hover over Robin, but made sure she could still see Luke's office door. After perusing the artwork on the walls in the receptionist area, she started to return to Robin's desk but froze.

"Hello, CJ."

Repulsion knotted inside of Christina's gut at the sight of Leroy Jones. Number one enemy of the Jenkins family and a man she loathed. He stood an arms-length away, and his sleazy gaze traveled the length of her body before returning to her face.

"Funny running into you here." He moved closer and Christina took a step back.

"Hello, Leroy." Disgust dripped from her words. She hadn't seen him in over a year, and now she wished it had been longer. Clean-shaven and wearing a suit still didn't hide the fact that he was a snake. With all of the headaches he had caused her family over the years, it took everything she had not to spit in his face. Instead, she turned and walked away without another word.

When Christina returned to Robin's desk, she chanced a glance over her shoulder and was surprised to see Leroy talking to Gary Rouse. It was never a good sign when two jackasses, who looked to be friendly, got together.

They walked toward the exit, but before they turned the corner, Leroy's gaze met hers. Christina gripped the bag of food tighter, wanting to look away, but she didn't. When he winked and flashed that stupid smirk, goosebumps covered her arms and nausea bubbled in her throat. The repugnance she felt toward him rose to a new level. *Scumbag.*

Luke's voice behind her caught her attention and she turned. He was standing near his office speaking with his client in the doorway.

"As I mentioned before, Miss Jenkins, Attorney Hayden has back to back meetings this afternoon. Maybe you can stop by another time," Robin said, trying to block Christina's view.

Too late. Luke had seen her.

He looked her over seductively as if she wasn't wearing her work clothes. His signature grin spread across his lips, and all thoughts of Leroy flew from her mind as her pulse picked up in speed. Christina didn't think she would ever get used to the way her body reacted with only a look from him.

He walked his client as far as Robin's desk and shook his

hand, promising to be in touch soon.

"Hey, baby. I'm glad you're here. Sorry to keep you waiting." His mouth swooped down over hers, and she melted into him, savoring his enticing kiss. It was probably a good thing her hands were full. Otherwise, she might have forgotten where she was and did something unspeakably erotic to him.

The sound of someone clearing their throat brought them both back to reality. Luke pulled away slightly but didn't remove his arm from around her.

"I'm starving," he whispered close to her ear and she knew he wasn't talking about food.

"Excuse me Attorney Hayden," Robin interrupted and glared at Christina, a be-prepared-to-leave-smirk plastered on her face. "Your next appointment should be here shortly."

Luke glanced at his watch. "Thanks, Robin. Until they get here, hold my calls." He took the bag of food from Christina and grabbed hold of her hand, guiding her to his office. Once there, he closed and locked the door.

"Now where were we?"

He set the bag on the table near the sofa and cupped her face between his strong hands, covering her mouth with his. A contented sigh slipped from her as Luke's tongue explored the inner recesses of her mouth. The kiss, slow and thoughtful, sent a wave of desire rushing through Christina's body, and she didn't want it to end. She took what he gave freely. Her arms went around his neck as she felt a sense of urgency with every swirl of his tongue, touch of his hand, and the feel of his body grinding against hers.

His hands scaled down the side of her body, his touch scorching her skin through the material of her clothing. No other man had ever turned her on the way Luke did, and Christina knew without a doubt that no other man ever would. His erection pressed against her stomach, and her need for him intensified.

"Ah, baby," he groaned into her mouth and lifted his

head, his breathing as ragged as hers. She took a step back. Her fingers touched her lips that were still warm and tingling from his kiss.

"That's not enough for me. I want more. I want you."

"I thought you were hungry." She played coy, knowing the look in his eyes told her exactly what he wanted.

"There's a battle going on within me. Part of me is starving since I didn't eat breakfast, but the other part of me prefers to taste you instead."

When he pulled her back into his arms, she placed her hands on his chest. "Tell you what. Why don't we eat first because I'm hungry too ... for food. Then we'll see how much time we have afterward."

After a slight hesitation, he agreed.

Sitting on the sofa, Christina pulled their meals out of the bag. The heady smell of onions, garlic, and basil, immediately greeted her when she took the lid from her lasagna, her mouth watered in anticipation.

They both moaned when the succulent spices hit their tongues.

"You were right, this is amazing."

"I'm glad you like it."

Christina had mentioned her favorite Italian restaurant on several occasions and decided he had to try the lasagna. When she told him she had a special treat for him for lunch, of course he initially thought she meant her.

"You're awfully quiet. Is anything wrong?" Luke asked between bites.

"I'm fine. While I was waiting for you, I saw someone that I knew talking to Gary. Someone who I wish would fall off the face of the earth."

"Wow, that bad huh?"

"Worse. I feel about him, the way you feel about Gary."

Luke shook his head and dabbed his mouth with the napkin in his hand. "That's impossible. You're too much of a sweetheart to have the same thoughts about that guy as I have about Gary."

"I don't know Lucas, my thoughts might surprise you. This guy used to work for Jenkins & Sons years ago and caused all types of trouble," she said between bites. "He really messed up and crossed the line when he attacked Toni."

"What?" Luke's mouth hung open, and his brows slanted in a frown. "When did this happen?"

"When she first met Craig." Christina told him how Toni had been doing plumbing work for Craig, and Leroy showed up at Craig's house. He found out she was there alone fixing a plumbing job that he had screwed up. They exchanged heated words, and he attacked her.

"You're shittin' me. If I were Craig, I probably would have killed that asshole."

"Trust me, he wanted to and probably would have if Toni hadn't been so shaken up by the experience. Instead of pummeling the guy, Craig called it in."

"Apparently this guy is not that bright, attempting to have his way with a woman, and then doing it at a detective's home. That's just plain stupid on so many levels."

"He's not known for being the smartest man in town. Or at least he wasn't when he worked for us. Now he's a general contractor and owns a small construction business. We hadn't heard anything from him until he tried to sue Jenkins & Sons, but nothing ever came of the bogus lawsuit."

"Well, hopefully, you guys won't hear from him again. As you mentioned earlier, maybe he'll fall off the face of the earth … and take Gary with him."

Christina laughed, knowing that she shouldn't wish something like that on anyone, but she couldn't help herself. She didn't like Leroy, and she didn't trust him.

Luke wiped his mouth with one of the napkins from the bag. "That was delicious, babe. Thanks for bringing lunch." He stuffed the empty containers back into the bag.

"You're welcome. I'm glad you had time for lunch since you often work right through." Christina popped a small piece of the garlic bread into her mouth before stuffing the rest into the trash.

"How much time do you have left?"

Christina shook her head and laughed. "You're insatiable."

"I'm in love."

Her heart fluttered like the wings of a bird. He had spoken those words many times before, but for some reason today they sounded different. They felt different. Maybe it was because he was leaving town later that night and wouldn't return for five days. Since getting back together, they had seen each other daily and Christina would miss him terribly.

"I'm in love with you too." She stood and reached for his hand. "I have about fifteen minutes before I have to leave. Maybe you can show me around your bathroom before your next appointment arrives."

"It would be my pleasure."

CHAPTER FOURTEEN

"Would you like to order a drink while you wait for your party?" the perky server asked Luke. Her Goth look: black clothing, black lipstick, and a shiny black mohawk, reminded him of one of many reasons he loved New York. People from around the world flocked to the city that was a melting pot of cultures, as well as personal styles.

"Yes. I'll have a Heineken and a glass of water."

"Alright, I'll be right back with your drinks."

"Thanks."

Luke glanced around his favorite pizza joint. The appetizing aroma of homemade bread, onions, garlic combined with a host of other scents of Tuscany had his stomach growling in anticipation. The food and the eclectic atmosphere made the establishment one of the most popular lunch spots in Midtown. His workload had once been so crazy busy that he didn't get to frequent the restaurant often, but ordered takeout weekly.

"Here you go." The server set down two coasters and placed his drinks in front of him. "Would you like to order or did you want to continue waiting for the other person in your party?"

"I'm a little early, so I'll wait."

He was meeting his friend, who was also a private investigator, Michael Cutter. Luke had hired him on a number of occasions to assist with his past cases. Unlike some P.I.'s, Michael dug deeper than most and could find a paperclip in a haystack. The guy had contacts in high and low places, able to get answers that no one else would think to look for.

After Christina's photo had ended up in a magazine regarding her Chicago show, Luke contacted Michael. Not only did he want answers about the photographer, he wanted to find out how the news got out about Sasha Knight. Since Luke knew he'd be in New York for a few days, he suggested they meet while he was in town.

Sitting next to the large picture window gave Luke a perfect view of the masses of people on the sidewalk rushing to get to their destinations. Horns blaring and people lifting their hands to hail taxis gave him a rush of New York adrenaline. The energy of the city was already seeping into his bones, and he had only been there two days.

Luke's cell phone vibrated in his pocket. A quick glance at the screen and a smile spread across his face.

"Hey, baby. I'm surprised to hear from you this time of day. Shouldn't you be elbow deep in paint right about now?"

"Yeah, but I couldn't stop thinking about you. I figured I'd give you a quick call and then maybe I can get some work done."

"It's good to hear your voice."

"You too. I also wanted us to agree to something."

"Oh boy. I'm almost afraid to ask." He never knew what to expect from her. "What is it?"

"We should have a rule that we can't be apart for more than three days."

Luke chuckled. "Now that's a deal I can agree too."

They talked for a few minutes, and his chest tightened thinking about how he fell in love with her more and more every day. He had also grown fond of the Jenkins family. Sunday brunches with them felt as normal as breathing, and he hadn't missed one in weeks. Also, bi-weekly outings with her male cousins and her brother were a regular occurrence. He couldn't believe how quickly her family had become the family he never had. If someone had told him a year ago that he would live in Cincinnati, be in love with an eccentric artist, and have intentions of marrying into a huge family, he wouldn't have believed them.

Luke glanced up and noticed his friend had walked in and was scanning the small restaurant. Luke waved him over.

"Hey, baby, Mike just walked in. Let me give you a call back a little later."

"Okay. I love you."

"I love you too." Luke pocketed his cell phone and stood.

"Well, well, well, if it isn't the prodigal son returning home." Michael grinned and stuck out his hand. He pulled Luke in for a one-arm hug and clapped him on the back of his shoulder.

"Only for a couple of days. So don't get used to seeing me."

Luke gave his longtime friend a once over. Often mistaken for Nick Cannon, he garnered attention wherever he went. He and Mike were about the same height, but Mike had at least twenty pounds on him, all muscle. A work out aficionado, it appeared his friend still hit the gym regularly.

"You're looking good, man." Luke gestured for him to have a seat across from him in one of the clunky wood chairs that had seen better days.

"It appears you've stepped up your workout unless you intentionally bought that T-shirt a size too small. Your arms are almost bigger than mine now."

Luke laughed glancing down at his navy blue Tee and bent his arm making his bicep pop. "Yeah, I've been doing a little somethin' somethin' now that I'm not working eighty hour weeks. I told you before, when I grow up I want to look like you. I figured I had better get started."

They talked and clowned for a few minutes before the server came over to take their order.

"I'm still trippin' you left all of this," Michael spread out his arms, "to live in the Midwest *and* you're still there. I thought, for sure, you would've moved back by now. So I guess the town is treating you well."

"Yeah, what can I say? My life is in Cincinnati now." The longer Luke lived in Ohio, the less he thought about New York. The relocation started out a little rocky, but he couldn't leave now. Not unless Christina was willing to go with him, and he was pretty sure she wouldn't move anywhere that was too far from her family.

"So who is she?"

"Who is who?"

"The woman you're in love with?"

Momentarily caught off guard, a slow smile covered Luke's lips. He lifted his beer bottle to his mouth and took a long drag from his beer, casting a glance across the table at his friend. No sense in denying anything. Michael was so good at what he did, he probably knew what Luke had for breakfast.

"Somehow I think you already know." Luke set his beer on the table.

Michael grinned without admitting anything.

"When I sent you a photo and asked that you look into the Chicago incident with the photographer—"

"I couldn't help myself." He shrugged. "I was curious. She's a beautiful woman."

"I agree, but how did you know that she and I were together?"

"I didn't." Luke narrowed his eyes. "At least not until you just admitted to it."

Luke shook his head and laughed. "I guess that's why you're the best P.I on the east coast."

Michael placed his hand over his heart. "Just the east

coast? Man, you wound me. You calling me instead of using someone else to dig up information for you must mean that I'm the best in the country."

"You're right. You're absolutely right. You're the best."

The server came over with their extra-large cheese and Italian sausage pizza. "Okay, here you go." The steam rising from the pie carried the pungent scent of roasted garlic, basil, sun-dried tomatoes, and jalapeno peppers that had Luke longing for a taste.

"Can I get you two anything else?"

"Maybe extra napkins," Mike said. They both dug into their meal the moment the server left the table.

"So what did you find?" Luke knew his friend. Michael Cutter never came back empty handed.

Michael opened his mouth to speak but stopped when the server returned with napkins. He waited until after she left before saying anything.

"According to my sources, the camera man took pictures of your woman during a show in New York."

"New York?"

Michael nodded. "Supposedly his boss found out about this artist who was on the verge of blowing up, but no one knew who she really was, and they started digging."

"Wait. When we saw him in Chicago, he mentioned that he knew who she was because of a reliable source. Any idea of who that might be?" Luke grabbed another slice of pizza. He had eaten the first slice so fast he barely remembered swallowing.

"Her agent, Valerie Cook."

Luke's hand stopped mid-air, the pizza slice an inch from his lips. "You're shittin' me."

"Nope. Valerie sent an anonymous email from a dummy account and apparently the magazine's tech department was able to trace it back to the source and found out the email came from her office."

Damn.

Luke knew the woman was up to no good, but he had no idea she would betray a client's trust this way. Now he had to break the news to Christina and wondered what she would do with the information.

"I appreciate you looking into this for me."

"Anything for you, man."

"What about that other situation?"

"Gary Rouse. Let me first start by saying that it looks as if someone else is investigating him."

Again, Luke was caught off guard, but then again, maybe he shouldn't be too surprised. Gary was a low-down, pompous jerk. Nothing should surprise Luke when it came to the guy. He had a feeling Gary probably had more enemies than friends.

"I haven't been able to find out yet who exactly is digging into his background, but my first guess would be a government agency, probably the FBI or CIA. They're digging deep."

"So were you able to find anything?"

"Yeah, he used to work for another law firm in Cleveland before he suddenly went to work for dear ol' dad."

"Really?"

Luke had never considered that Gary might have worked for any other firm than Atwater, Rouse & Stevenson, his father's firm.

"He probably would have still been there if he hadn't gotten himself into a little trouble. Well allegedly got himself into trouble. Years ago, he was investigated for stealing from client trust accounts and using the funds for personal use. The case never made it to trial. His father had hooked him up with a big shot attorney who poked holes in the case. Shortly after he was cleared, Gary joined Atwater, Rouse & Stevenson."

Luke would bet his life's savings that Gary had been guilty. "Anything else?"

Michael shook his head. "Not really. About two years

ago, there was some chatter about him taking money from clients, promising to perform legal services, but delivering nothing. I'll have to do a little more digging. It looks as if he's covering his tracks pretty good these days."

Luke sat back in his seat, twisting the now empty glass of water back and forth, dissecting all that Michael had told him. He didn't trust Gary, and he was glad to find out his suspicions weren't off.

"Does Gary have a law degree?"

Michael narrowed his eyes and folded his arms. "Why do you ask?"

Luke hesitated, wondering if he had hit on something. "The files he keeps on his cases look as if he doesn't know what he's doing. Most are incomplete. The ones that are complete are done either by one of the paralegals or a junior attorney." *Or by me*, Luke thought but didn't voice his thought. "So, does he have one?"

"Yeah, he has one. Although it took him three times to pass the bar."

"I see." Luke finished off his second slice of pizza and called the server over for more water.

"So, what are you going to do with this information?"

"I'm not sure yet. I might sit on it for a while since you're thinking he's currently being investigated. I'm a true believer that if you do wrong long enough, it'll come back to you in one way or another. I have a feeling Gary's going to get what's coming to him."

"I'm sure you're right." Michael pushed his plate aside and placed his used napkins on the table. "I'm surprised you haven't asked about that other situation."

"I figured if there were something to tell, you would've told me by now."

"You're right. I would have." He leaned forward and folded his hands on the table. "Right now, all is quiet with the Donati family. There's nothing that leads me to believe that they know you're related to Scott. If they do know, they don't see you as a threat. Of course, if anything comes up, you know I'll contact you."

Luke nodded. Now he had more than just his safety to consider. Christina was his number one priority, and he would never want any of his baggage to affect her. Ever! It gave him comfort in knowing that if the Donati family thought he knew anything, they would have acted immediately.

"Thanks, man. I appreciate everything you've done."

"We'll see if you'll be thanking me when you get my bill."

Luke laughed. "After all the info you've come up with, you have earned every single penny you're going to charge me. But can you give me the family discount?"

They both laughed, and Luke felt lucky to have some great people in his life. His biological family might be gone, but his longtime friends, the Jenkins family, and most importantly Christina, were all the family he needed.

*

John Legend's song, "All of Me," pumped through the conference room speakers where Christina was painting. The gentle melody washed over her like a lover's caress. The lyrics described what she was feeling these days perfectly. As a matter of fact, her life was perfect. The family finally knew about Sasha Knight, which was a weight off of her shoulders, giving her peace she hadn't felt in a long time. Her life with Luke was better than she could have ever imagined. In three weeks, they would be heading to St. Lucia for a much needed two-week vacation, and she could hardly wait.

Happiness whirled inside of her. Oh yeah, life couldn't get any better.

A smile crept across her lips. She couldn't go a few minutes without thinking about Luke and their last few months together. Phenomenal would be the best word to describe their relationship.

"You're starting to freak me out with that stupid grin on your face," her cousin Ben Jr. a.k.a. BJ said from the top of the six-foot ladder next to her. "So I take it things are good."

Christina stuck her paint roller in the pan on the floor and lapped up the taupe color paint. "Better than good. All is well in my world. What about you? How's that cutie-pie son of yours?" She used long strokes to spread the paint evenly over the walls, careful not to miss a spot.

"He is the coolest kid." Pride radiated from Ben and Christina could have sworn his chest stuck out more. "Fourteen months old and he's the smartest baby you'll ever meet. Every day it seems he does something that makes me wonder if he's a genius."

Christina laughed. "I heard you were like that when you were little too."

"Yeah, he's a chip off the old block."

"What about his mother?"

"What about her?"

"When are you going to marry her? You guys have been dating almost three years now."

Until recently, after Toni and Jada married, Christina hadn't thought much about getting married. But seeing how happy they were with their mates, she wanted to know what that felt like. One day.

"I'm not sure she's the one," BJ said, interrupting Christina's thoughts.

Christina halted the roller and lowered her pole to stare at her cousin. "Three years together and you two have a baby. How can you say she's not the right one? Why are you with her if she's not *the* one?"

"I thought she was the one, but now I'm not so sure. She's trying too hard to become a part of the Jenkins clan that it makes me wonder whether … Never mind about me. What about you? What's up with old boy, the thug lawyer?"

"Don't call him that!" She tried hiding her smile and started back painting. Some of her family, especially her male cousins thought Luke was *too cool* to be a lawyer.

"Speaking of lawyers. I'm surprised you weren't at the family meeting Thursday night. My dad announced that Leroy Jones is going through with the lawsuit against Jenkins & Sons."

"What?" I thought he didn't have a case." Christina had spent so much time with Luke, she hadn't realized how much she'd missed regarding the family. Her uncle Ben, BJ's father, was a lawyer and represented Jenkins & Sons.

"All right you guys, a little more work and a little less talk," Peyton said when she walked into the room with her clipboard.

"You're a regular slave driver, PJ. I'm tired of using my Saturdays for manual labor." BJ climbed down the ladder. He poured more paint into a smaller can before moving the ladder down the wall.

"Too bad. I'm going to need both of you for at least two more Saturdays. If you don't want the overtime, then I can see about giving you one of the weekdays off."

"PJ, why didn't you tell me about the lawsuit and that there was a family meeting this past Thursday?"

"First of all, you've been out of town or just missing in action. Secondly, I figured your boyfriend would tell you since Leroy is using his law firm."

Unease swept through Christina. *So that's why he was at Atwater, Rouse & Stevenson talking to Gary.* Luke had said nothing about his firm representing Leroy. As a matter of fact, Luke acted as if he had never heard of Leroy.

"By your silence I assume he didn't mention it."

"Maybe he doesn't know," BJ interjected. "There's probably a ton of lawyers at that firm with clients that Luke doesn't know."

Peyton's mouth tightened. She shot BJ a look that clearly said, "Butt out."

"Okay, you know what? I think this is a good time for me to take my fifteen minute break." BJ climbed back down the ladder and made a hasty retreat.

"He's right. Luke probably doesn't know otherwise I'm sure he would have mentioned something to me." Christina set her paint roller down, careful not to let the handle hit the wet wall. She poured more paint into her pan. "I can't believe we're being sued."

"Believe it. Leroy has some bogus claim that Jenkins & Sons has undercut his company five times in the past year, outbidding him. Supposedly, we have caused his business financial hardship, and he's claiming a whole lot of other crap."

"So what happens next?" Christina dunked her roller into the paint and went back to work.

Some of the crews had been remodeling Jenkins & Sons main office building, and repainting a few of the shops. She and Ben Jr. needed to finish the conference room before the day was over in order to start on the carpenter's shop Monday morning.

"I just heard from Uncle Ben and he said that Leroy's lawyer contacted him minutes ago. They want to meet Monday. Uncle Ben thinks they're going to try to settle out of court."

"Is that good?"

"I'm not sure. Grampa wants to be done with Leroy once, and for all. He said there's nothing to settle. So, we'll see what happens Monday."

"What time? I want to be there." She also planned to have a talk with Luke. Hopefully, he wasn't holding out on her. Unease settled in her gut like a paperweight. Despite what she had said to her sister, Christina wasn't a hundred percent sure Luke would have told her if he knew his office was representing Leroy.

"You can't attend the meeting. I'm not approving any more time off for you, especially since you'll be on vacation for a couple of weeks. More importantly, I need you here." She scanned the room. "We're already behind on the renovations thanks to all of your days off. Me, Grampa, and Uncle Ben will be the only ones there representing the company."

"I'm going Peyton."

"No, you're not." Peyton tucked her clipboard under her arm and pulled out her ChapStick, swiping it across her lips. "You need to quit being difficult. While you're trying so hard to get to this meeting, you need to be trying to figure out if your boyfriend has anything to do with this lawsuit. I'm sure your reason for wanting to be at that meeting has nothing to do with the lawsuit, but everything to do with seeing your boy-toy."

Ignoring the last part of Peyton's comment, Christina put more paint on her roller. She trusted Luke, but there was that little niggling of doubt brewing in the back of her mind. He didn't tell her everything, like when he failed to mention early in their relationship that he had a brother who had been killed.

She shook the doubt off. He would tell her if he knew anything. And so what if she did have other reasons for wanting to be at the meeting, like catching a glimpse of Luke. He'd been in New York for the last few days and wasn't expected back until Monday morning. Despite talking with him every day, she missed him like crazy. Sure she wanted to see him, but more importantly, she wanted to be there to represent the family.

"PJ, I'm not trying to be difficult. If anything, you're the one tripping. I don't need you to approve any time off since I can use my lunch break for the meeting. I'm a part of this family. I have a right to be there if I want to be. I don't know why you're making such a big deal about this."

"I could say the same thing about you. You have been unavailable for practically everything these last few months while you're pursuing your dreams and doing God knows what else. Were you thinking about the family then? Were you thinking about what all it takes to run this business?

Have you stepped in to attend any other meetings where we've had to *represent* the family and the business?"

Christina lowered her roller, tightly gripping the handle. She had no idea their conversation would take such a turn, a turn in the wrong direction.

"Another thing. You're so interested in helping the family, have you even taken the time to ask me if there is anything you can do to help out around here, to take some pressure off of me? No, you haven't. Your life is all about CJ. Now all of a sudden you want to be there for the family. Don't bother, Christina. We got this!" She turned and headed for the door.

"Now you just wait one minute!" Christina's voice wavered, anger punctuating each word. "First of all, I don't know what you're trying to imply by saying that I'm doing God knows what and I don't care. But how dare you suggest that I don't do anything or don't go the extra mile around here because I'm too busy pursuing *my* dreams. Have you forgotten that I was the first one to step in and help when you took over for Grampa?"

"No, I haven't forgotten, but that was—"

"I'm the one who was here day and night helping you make sense of that office and Grampa's crazy filing system. I'm the one who lent you a shoulder to cry on after those first few frustrating months when you were trying to get a handle on running the business. And I'm the one who filled in for you those weeks after your divorce. So forgive me if I've been taking some time for *me* lately. Taking some time to nurture *my* dreams." Irritation lodged in her throat, and she batted her eyes several times to keep tears from falling. The fact that her sister was teary eyed too wasn't helping.

They stood silent, both breathing hard with pent up emotion, the smooth melodies of Sam Smith now playing softly in the background. They had their share of disagreements, but none like this one.

Christina didn't know what to say. Disappointment and

frustration lay restless in her body. An electrician by trade, Peyton practically ran the business single handedly. No, Christina couldn't imagine the type of pressure her sister faced on a day-to-day basis. Nevertheless, she wasn't about to let Peyton or anyone else make her feel guilty about how she chose to spend her time or live her life.

"Hopefully you guys can finish this room today," Peyton said breaking the silence, her voice low and controlled. "Be sure to clean up before you leave." And with that, she walked away.

Christina's gaze followed her to the door. She might have been angry with Peyton, but it was clearer than ever that something was going on with her sister, and Christina had every intention of finding out what. She hated seeing her so unhappy, even if Peyton did get on her last nerve.

CHAPTER FIFTEEN

Luke nodded a greeting to a few familiar faces when he stepped into the mostly glass building that housed the law offices of Atwater, Rouse & Stevenson. It had been a helluva morning. The day was proving that the best-laid plans could change in a second. A thunderstorm on the east coast had delayed his flight to Cincinnati by three hours and then a flat tire on the way to the office didn't help. The only bright spot, he had plans of seeing Christina after work.

Luke stepped into the semi-crowded glass elevator. Glancing around a woman wearing too much perfume, he checked to make sure the button for the twelfth floor had been pushed. He moved to the rear of the car, and his mind immediately took him back to the conversation he'd had with Christina the day before. To say she was upset to learn that his firm was representing Leroy Jones would be an understatement. Unfortunately, he couldn't give her much comfort since he didn't know anything about the case.

When the elevator reached his floor, Luke maneuvered around three people in order to exit. "Excuse me," he said to a woman with an oversized bag that blocked his exit. He made a left, and when he reached their office suite, he took a deep breath before going in, mentally preparing himself for the day ahead.

"Welcome back, Luke," Robin greeted when he stepped up to her desk to retrieve his messages. Their working relationship had improved considerably after their conversation months ago.

"Thanks, Robin."

"I'm glad you're here. Anthony was just looking for you, not even five minutes ago." She handed Luke his messages. "I told him you should be here shortly and he said for you to come by his office before you get settled."

"Did he say what he wanted?" Luke flicked through the messages before stuffing all of them into the side pocket of his briefcase.

"Only that he needed you to take care of an issue for him."

Out of the senior partners, Luke liked Anthony Rouse, Gary's father, the least. He didn't trust the guy. And after meeting with Michael, Luke liked Gary and his father even less.

Luke and Robin discussed his afternoon appointments. Relieved to hear that two had cancelled, he headed down the hall thinking about what he would do with his two free hours.

Luke tapped on the open door of Attorney Rouse. "You wanted to see me, Anthony?"

"Oh Luke, come in. I'm glad you're here," he said in a rush, stuffing files into his briefcase. "Sorry to bombard you right when you walk in, but we're operating on a skeleton crew this afternoon. Come on, walk with me." He grabbed his suit jacket and shrugged into it before they left his office.

Luke stood back when the senior Rouse gave some parting instructions to his assistant, informing her that he wouldn't be available for the next three hours. A sudden bout of anxiousness swirled around in Luke's chest. He didn't know what this "issue" was that Rouse wanted him to take care of, but Luke knew he wasn't going to like whatever it was.

"Sorry about that, Luke. We have a client in Gary's office who needs our assistance. My son had a personal emergency and needed to leave." Anthony handed Luke a file. "Since he didn't want to cancel a meeting that's scheduled for eleven o'clock, which is in," he glanced at his watch, "fifteen minutes, he said you would be able to fill in for him."

A cold dread crept up Luke's spine and seeped into his bones. He had a feeling this meeting was the same meeting Christina had mentioned the night before. The meeting with Jenkins & Sons and Leroy Jones.

Luke and Rouse stepped out of the walkway and allowed one of the assistants to pass. Luke quickly skimmed through the documents. His bad morning just got worse. He closed the file and tried handing it back. Attorney Rouse stared at him, his brows slanted into a frown.

"I'm sorry, Anthony, but you're going to have to get someone else to handle this."

"Why? Gary said you wouldn't have a problem overseeing the meeting."

Heat rose to the back of Luke's neck as he barely controlled the scathing comment hanging on the end of his tongue. *Stay professional.* Luke's grip tightened on the manila folder.

"I'm not sure why Gary told you I'd be willing to fill in for him, but he was mistaken. I can't provide this client with diligent representation."

"And why is that?"

"Conflict of interest. I'm dating a member of the Jenkins family."

Anthony nodded. He still didn't take the file, and Luke was tempted to toss it into the nearest trash can. Normally if a lawyer expressed a conflict of interest, the ethical ramifications were taken seriously. Apparently not at Atwater, Rouse & Stevenson. Luke could think of other instances during his tenure where the firm hadn't always handled situations in the most principled way.

Rouse stepped forward, invading Luke's personal space. "Attorney Hayden, I'm sure I don't have to tell you how important our clients are to us. They pay us to provide them with legal representation, which is what you're going to do, even if it's just for today. You do whatever necessary to make our client feel that we're working on his behalf," he said in a low, controlled tone.

Luke's blood pressure rose steadily. It was at that moment he knew that would be his last day at Atwater, Rouse & Stevenson. There was no way in hell he would tolerate anyone treating him like some lackey, especially when he knew he didn't need the job or the money.

Maintaining eye contact with the older man, Luke thought of so many things he could say to him, like kiss my ass, or get your ignorant son to do his job. But Luke wouldn't stoop to that level. Instead, he would do what Rouse asked of him, but in the end, Gary and his father would regret the day they put him in this position.

Rouse took a step back and adjusted his suit jacket. "Since I have to be in court, I'll need you to follow through on this meeting with the client and the Jenkins family. At this point, I don't want Mr. Jones to have wasted a trip for something we couldn't control."

In other words, Rouse needed this meeting to happen so that the firm could still bill the client.

A short while later, Luke pulled out a copy of the Complaint that Gary had filed with the court on Leroy Jones' behalf. All he could do was shake his head as he skimmed the document and quickly went through the rest of the file astonished Gary thought they had a case.

"Attorney Hayden?"

Luke glanced up. His assistant stood in the doorway with a stout man he assumed was Leroy Jones. He had given her instructions to bring Leroy to his office right away.

Luke returned the documents to the file and stood. He stepped around his desk. "Mr. Jones." He shook the older man's hand. "I'm Luke Hayden."

"Nice to meet you," Leroy said enthusiastically.

"Thanks, Robin. That'll be all." Luke closed the door behind her and directed Leroy to one of the upholstered chairs in front of his desk. "All right, let's get started. We have a good five minutes before we have to meet with the Jenkins' lawyer."

"Attorney Rouse, well Attorney Gary Rouse, told me that you and he would be overseeing my case. He said you're one of the best lawyers here."

"Did he now?" Luke said tightly, the simmering anger in his gut was turning into a slow boil. "Unfortunately, Mr. Jones you have me at a disadvantage. I just received your information and only had a minute to bring myself up to speed, and so that you know, I won't be overseeing your case."

"But Attorney—"

"I'm only filling in with this meeting since it was too late for our firm to cancel."

Jones didn't seem too pleased at the turn of events, but Luke didn't care. As far as he was concerned, the lawsuit was a joke and Gary was dumber than Luke thought if he believed this would go anywhere.

Luke asked Leroy a series of questions about his construction business. Like how long he'd been in business. How many jobs had he lost to the Jenkins family? Why did he decide to go after the Jenkins family now?"

"I think they have some of these businesses in their pockets or something. There's no way they could keep beating me out of these jobs. They're underbidding and squeezing me out at every turn." Leroy's southern twang shined through.

Luke leaned back in his seat and steepled his fingers. "Mr. Jones, what made you think you had enough of a case to go after Jenkins & Sons?"

"I'd been thinking about it for a while. A friend of mine knows Attorney Rouse. He told him about my situation and Attorney Rouse called me."

Now this got Luke's attention. "So the lawsuit was Attorney Rouse's idea?"

Leroy hesitated. "Well, I guess, but I'd been thinking about it anyway. He said I definitely had a case." Leroy grinned, rubbing his hands together. "I'll finally be able to get back some of my money those thievin' Jenkins stole from me."

Luke stared at the older man who appeared to be mixed-race. He clearly had been running his hands through his brownish hair, the short strands sticking up and going in different directions. And his eyes. Luke had never met anyone with eyes that were such an unusual shade of blue with specks of gray. He also noticed Leroy couldn't hold his gaze for more than a few seconds before diverting his eyes.

Closing the file, Luke asked, "Did Attorney Rouse mention to you that the assault charges brought up against you a couple of years ago when you attacked one of the Jenkins' would—"

"Now wait a minute." Leroy's smug grin quickly dropped from his face. "I didn't attack her. It … it was a misunderstanding."

"Is that what they're calling it these days?" Luke spat out, unable to hold the words back. It took every bit of control he had not to say more. Before Leroy could respond, Luke stood. "All right, we'd better get going. I don't think it'll take long. This is just a preliminary meeting. I'm sure Attorney Rouse will be in touch with you regarding next steps. In the meantime, let's meet with the Jenkins' and let them know what you want."

Moments later, Luke and Leroy sat on one side of the conference table waiting for the Jenkins' to arrive. Luke remembered that Christina and Peyton had argued about her attending the meeting, and now he hoped Christina didn't show.

The conference room door swung open, and Luke stood as Ben Sr. walked in first. Steven Jenkins and Peyton followed. Ben Sr. and Steven greeted him with a friendly handshake, keeping the situation professional and not making it known that they knew Luke. Peyton was a different story. Her eyes narrowed, and her lips thinned with a cynical twist. She clearly wasn't pleased to see him. She took the seat on her grandfather's left, directly across from Luke.

Once everyone was seated, Luke started the meeting. "I'm glad you all were able to meet with us. Before we start, I want to inform you that I am *not* one of the lawyers on this case. Mr. Jones' lawyer had an emergency, and it was too late to contact all of you to postpone the meeting."

Christina's grandfather and uncle's expression remained friendly, and the tension lines on Peyton's forehead disappeared. Luke pulled a settlement-negotiating document from the file that Gary or someone on his team drew up with information about what Leroy was requesting.

"I'm not sure if you have received a copy of this," Luke said, sliding the document across the table to Ben, "but just in case you haven't."

Ben glanced at the information as he twirled an ink pen between his fingers. "We did get this information. Thanks for checking." He set the pen down. "Attorney Hayden, since this isn't your case, we'd prefer postponing until Attorney Rouse is—"

The door burst open, and Christina walked in.

"I'm so sorry I'm late, but ..." She froze.

Damn. Luke stood.

"How could you?" she snarled through gritted teeth, her eyes blazing. "I can't—"

"Christina." Her grandfather's warning tone caused her to clamp her mouth shut. Instead of saying more, she pulled the door open, slamming it against the wall, and stormed out of the room.

Peyton stood to go after her.

"Let me." Luke had Leroy follow him out of the conference room and Luke left him with Robin. Right now, he didn't care what the hell happened to Leroy or his lawsuit. All he wanted to do was get to Christina.

He caught up with her just as she passed his office and reached for her arm, but she snatched it away. "Christina, give me a chance to explain. Let's talk in my office." His words sounded calm, but fear gripped him like a noose around his neck. *I can't lose her.*

She stepped out of his reach but walked into the office.

The moment the door closed, she whirled on him. "I can't believe you acted as if you didn't know Leroy! Then you lied to me. You pretended not to know about the meeting. And not only are you in the meeting, but you're representing that asshole! How could you?"

"If you'll let me explain, you'll understand th—"

"No! I'll tell you what I understand. My family welcomed you, loved on you and pretty much adopted you, and this is how you thank them?"

"Christina—"

"My family would never betray you the way you're doing them. You have no idea how we have worked our *asses* off to build an empire that could withstand the test of time and be a legacy. Then some jerk comes along trying to sue for God knows what and you're helping him destroy us!"

"CJ, you're acting as if I'm attacking you and your family personally. This is a business situation that yo—"

"No!" She pointed at him, her eyes held so much anger, Luke knew she wouldn't be able to hear anything he had to say. "You made it personal when you went after my family!"

"Christina." He reached for her again but stopped when she backed away.

"I'm done. We're done!" She stormed out of the office.

Rubbing his hands down his face, he growled behind his palms. *This day just keeps getting worse.*

There was no sense in going after her. There was nothing he could say that she would hear, but there was something he could do. Adrenaline pumped through his veins as a plan that could get him disbarred slowly came together in his mind.

He set Leroy's file on his desk and pulled out his cell phone.

"What's up, man? Didn't I just see you?" Michael asked by way of greeting.

Luke fingered the file in front of him. "I need your help with something ... and I need it like yesterday."

CHAPTER SIXTEEN

Christina paced the length of Peyton's office like a caged animal. She so wanted to believe Luke didn't know about the meeting. *But I know what I saw.* How could he go after her family?

CJ, if you give me a chance to explain.

His words volleyed around in her head. She had been too angry and shocked to hear anything he had to say. She couldn't even remember how she arrived back at work.

The door to the office swung open, and Peyton stopped midstride upon seeing Christina, but recovered quickly.

"You put on quite the little show this morning." Peyton set her large purse that doubled as a laptop bag into the chair next to her desk. Shrugging out of her short black suit jacket, she draped it over the back of the same chair before she sat behind her desk. "I'm not even sure what to say to you."

"I'm sorry," Christina said. "I should have listened to you about Luke and I should have stayed at work instead of barging into the meeting. I thought I could trust him, PJ. I can't believe he would represent Leroy, especially knowing how our family feels about the guy."

Peyton's brows drew together, and she leaned forward in

her seat. "What are you talking about? Luke isn't the lawyer on the case. Didn't he tell you that when he went after you?"

Dread washed over Christina like a tsunami crashing onto the shore, wiping everything out in its wake. She wasn't sure whether to be happy at finding out that Luke wasn't representing Leroy or whether to cry. *Oh my God. What have I done?*

Christina dropped down in the chair. "What do you mean?" she croaked, almost afraid to receive the answer to her question.

"If you had stuck around or given Luke a chance to explain, you would have known his boss asked him to fill in for another lawyer, Gary somebody, at the last minute. From what I understand, Luke had just arrived back in town. He didn't even know what the case was about, or who the parties were until minutes before he walked into that meeting room."

A sick feeling swirled inside Christina's gut. How could she have thought the worst of him? She claimed to love him. How could she not listen to him when he tried to explain?

"I just ..." Christina couldn't get her words together. "When I saw him sitting at the table, I couldn't believe it. I was shocked. You guys must have been surprised to see him too."

"You have no idea. My first reaction was similar to yours, but Grampa gave me that look. You know the one. The one that says sit down and be quiet."

"Yeah, I know the look. I've received it plenty of times," Christina said absently, still playing the scene around in her mind. She groaned and put her head in her hands. "That's why Grampa hushed me. He was trying to tell me that things weren't as they seemed."

"I'm glad I kept my mouth closed," Peyton said. "Those first few minutes were awkward, but when Luke explained why he was there. I calmed down. I actually felt bad for him. After you had left, I got the impression Luke had been blindsided by the meeting. When he came back into the conference room after dealing with you, the tension bouncing off of him was fierce."

Christina thought of Gary. If that guy was up to no good, God help him when Luke got his hands on him. Then again, that scared Christina even more. Luke was probably already angry with having to fill in for Gary, and she hadn't helped matters by overreacting and verbally attacking him.

"What am I going to do? He probably hates me," Christina said behind her hands.

She recalled every mean thing she had said to him, and she would never forget the hurt in his eyes. "He's never going to forgive me."

Peyton stood and walked over to the single window in her office and opened the blinds.

"CJ, I know I've given you a hard time about Luke," she said, her back to Christina. "But I was wrong. I've been wrong about so many things lately. I'm not sure where to start with my apologies." She finally turned.

Christina stood next to the desk, toying with the pencil holder that was made to look like an electrical box. Their grandfather had given the custom piece to Peyton after she finished her electrician apprenticeship.

"You don't have to apologize," Christina said. "I have said some things to you that I'm not proud of either."

"You didn't say anything that wasn't true."

"Well … the things I said behind your back might not have been true." Her lips quirked trying to hide a smile.

Peyton frowned, but Christina didn't miss the humor in her eyes. "Oh. I'm sure I don't want to know what you said behind my back." She turned fully to Christina. "I really am sorry about everything. I hate when we fight. As for Luke, he seemed pretty upset this morning. Actually, I don't know if upset is the right word. I think he was more pissed than anything, and I don't think it had anything to do with you. At least not at first. Even sitting in the meeting, he seemed on edge."

Peyton filled Christina in on the brief meeting and the tension in the room. Luke had informed them that Gary was the lawyer for the case and would contact them soon.

Christina didn't know how or what she would say to make things right with Luke. But she had to try. She couldn't lose him again.

*

Two days later, Christina knocked on her grandfather's partially opened office door.

"Can I come in?"

The elder Jenkins looked up from the book he was reading, his glasses perched on the tip of his nose. She wondered how he could stand to wear those glasses like that when it looked so uncomfortable.

"Of course, sweetheart. Come on in." He set the book to the side, placing his glasses on top.

Christina walked farther into the office. The only light in the room was that of the floor lamp next to her grandfather's favorite chair, which he occupied. Shaking out of her lightweight jacket, she laid it on the sofa along with her bag, before taking a seat.

Now that she had her grandfather's attention, words failed her.

"How's the painting going?" Her grandfather asked, filling the silence.

Thankful for the momentary distraction, Christina was reminded of what Luke had found out while in New York. She couldn't believe Valerie would betray her and for what? To sell more paintings? Christina still wasn't buying the woman's reasons, and it didn't matter. They were no longer working together.

"The paintings are going well," she finally answered. "I'm slowing things down a little since I won't be doing a show in a while."

"And what about Luke?"

Christina hesitated. "I think I really blew it this time, Grampa." She kicked off her tennis shoes and tucked her feet underneath her butt. "I don't know if he'll ever forgive me for jumping to conclusions and for not giving him a chance to explain."

"You're young. I can't begin to tell you about all the misunderstandings your grandmother, and I had early in our relationship. You girls took those fiery tempers after Katherine. She used to give me hell." He laughed.

Christina smiled. Her grandmother had shared plenty of stories and insisted that the majority of their disagreements were CJ's grandfather's fault. Katherine Jenkins still didn't play, but what Christina loved most about them is that no matter how mad they might get at each other, they never went to bed angry. That's what she wanted. That's what she wanted with Luke.

"I don't know what to do about Luke."

Sadness swelled in her heart. If she weren't such a chicken, she would have called him that same day and apologized to him. Even if he didn't want anything else to do with her, she at least owed him that much. Until recently, her temper rarely reared its wicked head. It usually took a lot to get her angry and within days, she had spat hateful words at both Peyton and Luke, two people she loved dearly.

"I can't believe how I behaved, especially since I know Luke. He has more integrity in his pinky finger than most people have in their whole body. Grampa I didn't give him a chance to explain. All I could think about was that he was going up against our family."

"I don't know what it is with you girls. You get these great guys and then you find a way to push them away. I'm starting to see a pattern. First Toni, then Jada and now you."

Christina couldn't speak for her cousins, but she didn't intentionally push Luke away. She guessed it didn't matter though. Intentionally or unintentionally, she had still screwed up the best thing that had ever happened to her.

"I blame myself for some of this," her grandfather said.

"Why? You didn't do anything."

"I'm the one who instilled in all of you, from an early age, the importance of putting family first, but I think I need to add more to that speech now."

Christina's shoulders sagged knowing one of her grandfather's speeches could take hours, but then again, she was desperate. He had never steered her wrong, and she hoped he could say something that would help her situation.

"Once you commit your life to a man, a good man, then he should be your top priority. Hopefully you'll never have to choose your mate over your family or vice versa, but if ever you are in that position, you should side with your mate."

"What if he's wrong? I'm not saying that's the case here, but I'm sure when I do get married, my husband is not going to always be right."

"Probably not, but you'll work together to get the right answer. Christina, don't risk losing Luke out of some loyalty to the family. Besides, I think Luke might have showed some loyalty to the Jenkins family."

Christina tilted her head. "How so?"

"I talked with your uncle Ben earlier regarding this mess with Leroy and Ben received some interesting information. Well good news for us, but not for Leroy."

"What news?"

"Though your uncle never thought Leroy had a case, someone sent Ben some anonymous information that could have put Leroy away for years if Ben had a chance to use it. But he didn't have a chance. Leroy was picked up on bribery charges this afternoon."

"What? How?"

"From what I understand, the Department of Investigation and the District Attorney's office has been investigating scheming contractors who have been bribing city inspectors. According to Ben, some of the inspectors have been rushing through projects and signing off on permits without the work being properly done." Her grandfather leaned forward, his elbows on his thighs. "Yesterday, they received photos of Leroy offering a bribe and a signed statement from a city inspector confirming this."

"And you think Luke sent the information to the District Attorney and Uncle Ben?"

Her grandfather hesitated. "The information was sent anonymously, but Ben thinks the timing is too much of a coincident. He believes your boyfriend had something to do with the chain of events."

"Well, he's probably my ex-boyfriend. Luke is never going to forgive me." She had let him down once by not being honest with him and trusting him with her secret, and this time her distrust reared its ugly head again.

"He'll forgive you."

Christina looked at her grandfather sideways, trying not to get excited, but hoped he knew something she didn't know. She placed her feet on the floor and sat forward. He had spoken the words with such authority. He had to know something. "How can you be so sure?"

"Because he's in love with you."

Christina dropped her shoulders and sat back. "I don't know if love is enough this time, Grampa."

"It's enough, but you'll never know if you keep hiding out at home, or over Jada's house, or even over here. Instead of talking to all of us, you need to be talking to Luke. He's probably missing you as much as you're missing him, but you're the one who has to make this right."

Christina knew her grandfather was right. She was a grown woman. It was time she started acting like one.

"By the way, I heard he quit his job."

"Wha ... what?" Christina brought her hands up to her mouth. *God, please don't let him have moved back to New York or worse, gotten into trouble because of me.*

181

*

Luke lounged on his sofa, flipping through TV channels trying to find a baseball game. Out of all of the professional sports, he liked baseball the least, except during the playoffs.

Finally settling on a channel, he tossed the remote to the side, rested his head against the back of the sofa, and propped his legs on the coffee table. The position had become a norm for him in the last two days, each day felt longer than the last.

Most people who up and quit their jobs usually either have something lined up or start searching for something new right away. Not Luke. He needed time to regroup. Time to reevaluate his life, as well as his plans for the future, and he couldn't think about his future without thinking about Christina. When they reunited months ago, he had promised himself that he would never let her go again, and he meant it. She didn't know, but he knew there was no one else for him. He planned to spend the rest of his life with her.

Planting his feet on the floor, Luke stood and walked over to his doublewide, stainless steel refrigerator. Holding the door open and peering in, he considered cooking, but quickly shot that idea down. Instead, he grabbed a beer and went back to the sofa. At some point, he was going to have to do something other than watch television, and drink beer camped out on the sofa. But for now, kicking back was working for him.

He brought the bottle to his lips but stopped before he could take a swig when his cell phone vibrated on the table. Holding the bottle in one hand, he picked up the phone with his free hand. Glancing at the screen, he sat forward and set the beer down when he saw that it was a text from Christina.

"Is it a crime to fight for what is mine?"

A slow smile spread across Luke's face. *When did she start quoting Tupac?* Hell, he didn't care who she quoted as long as he was hearing from her.

Don't think so, but if it is, I know a good lawyer.

I know one too…

Luke wanted to see her more than anything, despite still being a little pissed that she didn't trust him. The day she accused him of lying and of going after her family hurt more than he would ever admit. After all, they'd been through, and all the time they'd spent together, she should have known he would never do anything to hurt her or the Jenkins family.

Without a doubt, they needed to talk. She needed to understand a few things, and he needed to see her. Hold her.

He went back to his cell phone.

In case you plan to commit a crime, contact your lawyer first.

When minutes passed, and he didn't receive a text back, he picked up the cigarette that he'd been ogling all day. He twirled it between his fingers. He hadn't had a smoke in weeks and tonight he craved one almost as much as he craved having Christina in his arms.

He laid his head against the back of the sofa and closed his eyes. For a minute, a flutter of eagerness bounced around in his gut at hearing from her. He was acting like a damn high school boy getting all excited about hearing from the most popular girl. What had his life come to that a woman held this type of power over him?

He stuck the cigarette in his mouth, letting it dangle from his lips. The only thing that kept him from lighting up was his promise to Christina. He wouldn't go back on his word.

Releasing a low groan, he sat up straight and tossed the cigarette on the table. This is ridiculous. *I need to get out of here.*

Luke slipped on his sneakers and grabbed the keys from the kitchen counter. He had no idea where he was going, but he would drive until he got there. When he went back to the coffee table, he lifted the remote to turn off the television, but froze. A photo of Gary and the outside of Atwater, Rouse & Stevenson displayed across the screen.

"This just in. Attorney Gary Rouse of the law firm Atwater, Rouse & Stevenson has just been arrested on charges of conspiracy to commit money-laundering, conspiracy to commit wire fraud, and tax evasion," the news reporter said. *"You might remember twenty years ago, three other attorneys at this same law firm were arrested on similar charges and one of those individuals committed suicide while on bail. According to our sources, the firm is being investigated, but so far only Attorney Rouse has been arrested. He will ..."*

Luke pumped his fist in the air as satisfaction stormed through his veins. He only wished he could have been there to watch the cops drag Gary's sorry ass off to jail.

"The District Attorney's office received anonymous information this morning..."

A soft knock sounded on Luke's door, and he reluctantly pulled his attention from the television, wanting to hear what else the news reporter had to say.

He dropped the remote on the sofa and hurried across the room. When he swung the door open, his heart stuttered. Excitement washed over him, and he gripped the doorframe at the sight of Christina standing on the other side of the threshold looking sexy as hell.

Her wild hair was piled on top of her head, and though she didn't need makeup, he liked how exotic her eyes looked with the dark eyeliner. And those lips. He couldn't wait to smear the lipstick covering her tempting lips. His gaze traveled lower to the outfit, which was so unlike her, but Luke had to admit he liked what he saw. The fuchsia, button down blouse, brought out the colors in her cheeks, and surprisingly she had on a bra. He knew this because a hint of pink lace peeked out from the top of her blouse where she had left the top four buttons undone. His body stirred as his eyes went lower to the skintight black jeans and the fuck-me pumps.

Luke had never been so happy to see someone in his life.

He closed the distance between them. Instead of wasting time talking, he cupped her face between his hands and lowered his mouth to hers. At that moment, the frustration from earlier crawled to the back of his mind. He didn't care that they still had things to work out. All he wanted was to feel her body against his and taste her sweet lips.

Her arms looped around his neck, and he lowered his hands to her butt that fit perfectly in his grip. Pulling her close, he took what he wanted, not caring that they were standing in the hallway. All he cared about was that his woman was there with him, where she belonged.

If Luke hadn't heard the ding of the elevator, he would have kept kissing Christina. Reluctantly he lifted his mouth from hers and stared into her eyes. He hadn't kissed her in seven days, not since their lives had stalled the day he returned from his New York trip.

"I'm sorry," she whispered before he could form any intelligent words. "I'm so sorry."

He gave a slight nod, unable to tear his gaze from hers. He reached for her hand and backed them into his condo, shutting the door with his free hand.

"Please say something," Christina said, anxiousness in her voice.

"Since I can't say those four words we vowed never to say again, I'm not sure what to say."

Her beautiful mouth curved into a smile, her eyes gleaming with love. "I'm glad you didn't say the words, but I know we have to talk."

He led her to the sofa. "Ahh, Lucas, I thought you quit." She scoffed at the pack of cigarettes he had tossed on the sofa table.

"I did."

"Then what is this all about?" She waved the pack in the air. "If you quit, you shouldn't need these."

Luke released a breath and dropped down on the sofa. "I did quit and I almost needed those because I didn't have you." She cringed at the bite in his words, but she needed to hear them. She needed to remember why they were tiptoeing around a conversation that they should have had days ago.

"I'm sorry." She placed the cigarettes back on the table and sat on the sofa. "I have no right to come in here and tell you what you should or shouldn't do."

"Actually, you do have the right. You have every right to question me about anything in my life." He turned to her. "Just because you've been keeping your distance these last couple of days doesn't mean that I stopped loving you. I love you so damn much. I couldn't stop even if I wanted to."

"Lucas. I love you too, but I don't know how you can ever forgive me for thinking the worst of you. I will never be able to apologize enough for my behavior, for all that I said and most importantly, for doubting your love. I'm so sorry."

He placed a lingering kiss against her temple, thankful to have her close. "I'm sorry too, but if we're going to have a future together, there's some things we need to get straight."

"I know," she said softly.

"This disappearing for almost two days can't happen again. If we have a problem, we're going to talk about it like adults until we work it out." Luke knew that he could have gone to her just as easily, but he thought it best that she came to him when she was ready to talk, as well as listen.

"Yeah … you're right. I guess I was caught off guard that morning. When I walked into that conference room, you were the last person I expected to see."

Luke sat back and pulled her against his body. "I know. I'm sure the situation appeared incriminating."

"But you tried to explain. I hate that I didn't give you a chance. I immediately thought the worst instead of giving you an opportunity to tell me what was going on."

"Baby, that's why we have to make sure we keep the lines of communication open." He ran his hand up and down her arm. "Maybe I shouldn't have assumed you knew this, but I will always be honest with you. You're the most important person in my life. Don't ever doubt my love for you or the lengths I will go to make you happy. But with that, I need to know that you'll be honest with me. Whatever it is, good or bad, I have to know that you'll be straight with me."

She lifted her head from his shoulder but kept her arms around his waist. "Always. No more secrets. No more of me jumping to conclusions. I will always talk to you *and* listen. I love you so much, and I have so missed you. Do you realize we haven't been together in almost eight days?"

He brushed a gentle kiss across her lips. "Trust me, I know. Going forward, I don't plan to spend any days away from you."

"I'm glad to hear that. I feel the same way." Christina placed her hand on top of his, which was sitting on her thigh. "I heard you quit your job."

Luke nodded. "It was time."

Silence fell between them until Christina said, "Do you want to talk about it?"

"No." She probably expected a different response, but he honestly didn't want to talk about that day. At the time, it seemed he couldn't get out of that building fast enough. Now in light of the recent news, he left right on time. Luke knew as a recent former attorney with the firm, he would be questioned during the investigation, but he'd be ready.

When Christina didn't say anything else, Luke glanced down at her. The corners of her lips lifted and a sexy smile spread across her mouth.

"I'm okay with us not talking about it. I can think of something else I'd rather do."

"Really?"

"Mmm hmm." Her hand started at his stomach and inched up his chest, stopping at one of his nipples. Heat spread through his T-shirt as if she had made contact directly to his skin. "Do you happen to have any R. Kelly tunes hanging around?"

She tweaked the other nipple, and he practically leaped off the sofa.

"Later for R. Kelly." Luke lifted her in one smooth swoop and carried her toward his bedroom. "Tonight, we'll make our own music."

"Wait!" Luke stopped in his tracks and glanced down at her. Wait – the same word she'd spoken their last night in New York. He hoped there weren't any more secrets that she was planning to share. "Did you send my uncle pictures of Leroy paying off some city inspectors?"

Luke hesitated. "What pictures?"

He stood in the middle of the hallway still holding Christina in his arms as she searched his eyes. He wasn't sure if she was trying to determine whether or not he knew more than what he was saying or if she was trying to think of another question.

Instead of saying anything, she placed one of her hands behind his head and gently pulled him toward her. Heat coursed through his body, and he lost himself in the sweetness of her lips. Luke knew they still had some growing to do as a couple, but he loved her more than words could ever express. She meant everything to him. From this moment forward, he planned to do whatever it took to keep her in his life. Forever.

EPILOGUE

Three weeks later

Christina dug through the Coach Hobo bag for her wallet as the taxi driver pulled into the parking lot of Teddy's Bar and Grill. She couldn't wait to see her cousins. With most of them having significant others now, they didn't hang out as much.

"Thanks." She handed the driver a few bills before exiting the car.

A warm tingling sensation heated Christina's body in thinking about her significant other. Prior to their vacation, she and Luke had moved in together. Since they spent so much time at each other's place, they agreed living together was the most logical thing to do at this point in their relationship. She chuckled to herself when Luke had told her that the first order of business was to get that death trap she called an elevator converted to a real elevator.

Between moving Luke in and their recent vacation, Christina felt on top of the world. St. Lucia was beautiful with the bluest water and white sand beaches as far as the eye could see. Sunshine had been in abundance and the perfect temperature had Christina wanting to stay there forever. The only real surprise of the trip came the first day they arrived. They were touring the resort and wandered into the pool area. To their amazement, women roamed around with their breasts hanging free and their other goodies on display. Even some men bared all, flexing what their mommas gave them, and no one seemed to care. Neither she nor Luke knew clothing was optional when booking the vacation and Christina could honestly say that the trip as a whole was an experience she wouldn't soon forget.

Christina hurried into the bar. As usual, she was late.

"Well it's about time," Martina said and bit into a big juicy burger, grease running down the side of her chin. "We were starting to think that maybe you weren't back in town yet."

Christina couldn't stop staring at her cousin's double-decker sandwich. She had been dreaming about burgers for months, trying not to succumb to the temptation, but dreaming nonetheless.

"I see you were able to get some sun. Your skin is absolutely glowing. When did you get back?" Peyton asked.

"Thanks. We arrived last night." Christina still couldn't seem to take her gaze off the two-handed burger Martina set back on the plate. Usually, she could ignore most of the foods her cousins ate that didn't fall in line with her vegetarian food regimen. But tonight was proving to be a bit harder than usual. "Where's Jada and Toni?"

"Jada and Zack are in Boston and Toni is at home with little Craig. She called and canceled saying Craig Jr. has a bad cold."

"Aww, I'm sorry to hear that. Hopefully, he'll feel better soon."

Martina took another bite of her hamburger. Her eyes slid closed and with the sensual moans she made with every chew, one would think she was in the throes of passion. It was then Christina knew her cousin was intentionally trying to torture her.

Martina opened her eyes, and her gaze met Christina's. "Good grief. Just order a damn burger already and quit staring at mine."

"Why, so you can talk about me? I don't think so." Christina finally looked away and grabbed a menu from the edge of the table.

"I'm going to talk about you anyway." Martina bit into her burger again, still acting as if it were the best meal she had ever eaten.

Unfortunately, her taunting worked. Christina perused the menu with every intention of ordering the biggest, greasiest, coma-inducing burger the bar had. No longer would she deprive herself of re-experiencing the delectable taste that at one time made her toes curl. So what if Martina teased her. As long as her cousin was picking on her, then she was leaving someone else alone.

Christina waved the server over and ordered a burger and fries. She rolled her eyes when Martina started in on her. Reminding her that being a vegetarian for a limited amount of time could be added to her list of failed attempts.

"Okay, enough," Peyton nudged Martina in the side with her elbow. "I want to hear CJ's big news."

Christina's brows drew together. "What big news?"

"You might as well tell us, we're going to find out eventually anyway." Peyton took a sip from her glass of wine.

Christina shook her head and shrugged. "For real. I don't know what you're talking about."

"I think she's serious." Martina wiped her mouth and tossed her soiled napkin onto her empty plate.

"We assumed you and Luke would come back married."

"What? Uh, nooo." Christina wiggled her bare ring finger.

"Were you disappointed?" Peyton asked.

"Not at all. Marriage wasn't even mentioned on this trip."

Luke might not have mentioned marriage while on

vacation, but over the last couple of months, he had made comments about them someday marrying. Saying things like: "How long would you want to be engaged?", "What do you think about us relocating once we get married?", "When we start a family ..." And those were only a few mentions.

In her heart, Christina knew she would marry him in a heartbeat should he ask, but in reality, she wasn't ready for marriage. She loved Luke more than she thought possible, and he was excellent marriage material. But after her behavior in his office weeks earlier, she achingly realized she still had some growing up to do. She claimed to trust Luke, but that afternoon said otherwise.

"For a minute there, I thought you were trying to pull a fast one over on us like you did with *Sasha Knight*. I still can't believe you paint nudes and Gram and Grampa haven't kicked you out of the family," Martina said.

"Oh please. If they haven't kicked you out yet, there's no threat of them doing that to me." Only a few months ago, Christina had the same thoughts as Martina. But the news of her being Sasha Knight went over much better than Christina had anticipated. Her parents were a little surprised by the nudes but proud of her success as were other members of the family.

"I heard Uncle Ben offered your man a job," Peyton said cutting into Christina's thoughts.

"Yep, he made the offer the day before we left." The server placed Christina's meal in front of her along with a Sprite.

"So is he going to accept?" MJ asked.

"I don't know he hasn't said."

When Luke quit his job at Atwater, Rouse & Stevenson, Christina was afraid he planned to move back to New York. He had never mentioned going back, but every month he seemed to get a call from a law firm offering him a job.

While on vacation, she asked him if he were planning to go back. He answered with a question. He asked whether or not she would go with him if he did decide to move back to New York. Without having to think, she said yes. She recalled his shock. He had pulled her into his chest, told her how much he loved her and that he had no intention of leaving Cincinnati, knowing how important family was to her.

"Alright, you guys. I'm out of here." Martina stood and slipped into her jacket. She glanced at the food bill and dropped some cash on the table.

"Don't forget about the breakfast meeting tomorrow downtown," Peyton said. "Wear something nice. You don't have to wear a dress, but at least wear a nice pantsuit. We'll be schmoozing with some big-time business people."

"Then why are you taking MJ," Christina asked, having a hard time keeping her smile at bay.

"Forget you future Mrs. Thug Lawyer."

"Don't call him that!"

"I know you're not try—"

"Would you two stop?" Peyton nudged them both. "MJ, just promise me you're going to be there and that you're not going to wear some old, ripped jeans and steel toe boots."

"Yeah, yeah, I'll be there." Martina pulled Christina's hair when she walked passed.

Christina shook her head and smiled. If Martina behaved any other way, she would think something was wrong.

"How did you talk MJ into attending that breakfast with you? Isn't Senator Paul Kendricks the guest speaker at that event?"

Peyton nodded and frowned, her lips pursed tightly.

Martina would rather eat nails than even hear the name – Paul Kendricks. She thought he was the lowest form of human life and often referred to the senator as Satan's spawn. Kendricks was against the trade unions, and Martina had spent most of her carpenter career as an advocate for the unions.

"The senator is the speaker, but I didn't tell her."

Christina finished chewing and then threw her head back and laughed. "You're going to be sorry."

"I know," Peyton whined, covering her face with her hands. "I wanted at least two of us representing Jenkins & Sons. Nick was going to attend, but he and his crew have to install a furnace this weekend for a new client."

"Since he'll be working the whole weekend, and you were just getting back into town, I thought of MJ."

"She is going to totally flip at that meeting."

"That's why I'm going to have Craig and Uncle Ben on speed dial, just in case."

Having a police detective and a lawyer in the wings probably wasn't a bad idea.

"Is Luke still meeting you here?" Peyton placed the money for her meal on top of Martina's.

"Yes, he should be here any minute now." Christina rubbed her stomach feeling nauseous. Maybe she shouldn't have eaten the whole burger.

"I'm glad we have a few minutes alone. I wanted to talk to you, to apologize. I know I've been a pain to deal with lately, and I'm sorry ... for everything."

"PJ, you don't have to keep bringing it up. We've already settled our differences."

Before they had left on their trip, Peyton had invited Christina and Luke over to her house for dinner so she could apologize.

"So what's been going on?" Christina asked. She never had a chance to find out why Peyton had been so unhappy.

Her sister's gaze traveled around the bar, before returning her attention to Christina.

"I'm not sure. I think a combination of things. I'm tired, CJ. I'm tired of my life, the way it is. So instead of me taking some much needed time off, I've been taking my frustrations out on everyone around me."

"Is there anything I can do?"

"I'll probably need your help in the office next month

when I go on vacation. Other than that, I should be able to handle everything."

"Do you want to talk about what's been frustrating you?"

Peyton shook her head. "There's just some things I need to work through on my own."

"Does it have anything to do with Dylan?" Christina asked, taking a chance on mentioning Peyton's ex-husband.

"Indirectly. When we broke up, it left a void in my life. I have felt empty ever since. Don't get me wrong, I have no intention of getting back with him, but there are some things I do miss about not being a couple anymore."

Peyton told her how weird it was trying to make new friends and start over. She and Dylan did a lot as a couple, and most of their friends were married. So after the divorce, she felt as if they either had to split up their friends or move on all together and not hang out with them. Peyton also talked about how empty her house felt. She received the house in the divorce settlement. Instead of selling the four bedroom, three bathroom home, she had decided to stay.

"Well, it looks like Luke just arrived." Peyton stood and slipped on her jacket. "Thanks for listening and don't worry about me. I'll get myself together. I always do."

She watched her sister walk up to Luke and greet him with a hug before leaving. Christina smiled to herself, so glad they were finally getting along.

"Hey, baby. You ready to go?" Luke bent down and kissed her.

"Yep, I'm ready. Do you want to order anything to take home?"

"Nah, I'm good. Did you already pay for your meal?" he asked, his money clip in his hand.

"Not yet."

After a quick glance at her bill, Luke tossed two twenties on the table, more than covering her portion of the bill.

Christina stood and wobbled on her legs, clutching her stomach. "God I feel sick."

Luke held onto her elbow. "Were you drinking?"

"Nothing but soda."

"And what did you eat?" Concern spread across his face.

"A bacon cheeseburger with steak fries."

Luke stared at her, and Christina understood the look. She couldn't believe that after almost a year of being a vegetarian, she'd ruin her mission by indulging in a burger and not just any burger.

"You're kidding right?"

She shook her head, wishing she were.

"Baby, you can't go from eating lettuce and tomatoes for almost a year to eating a pound of beef. No wonder your stomach is protesting." He rubbed her belly.

Normally his touch anywhere on her body sent tingles of desire to every cell, but not tonight. "I'm going to be sick." She darted off to the bathroom clutching her stomach, her hand clasped tightly over her mouth.

She rushed into the dingy, two-stall restroom and barely made it to the toilet before the contents of her stomach declared war. Each time she thought she couldn't possibly have anything left to throw up, her stomach rolled again, and bile rose in her throat.

Christina didn't know how long she hugged the toilet, but it must have been long enough for Luke to be concerned.

"CJ?" He called in the distance. She could only hope he was standing at the door and hadn't walked into a ladies' room. It sounded as if she were the only one in there, but she still didn't think it was a good idea for him to be there.

"Christina?" His voice was closer.

"In here," she said, barely hearing her own voice and doubting he heard her.

The sound of water flowed from the faucet, and then the electronic towel holder whined.

Too weak to do anything else, she dropped on her butt and leaned against the white subway tile lining the wall. Her eyes barely open, she noticed when the door to the handicap stall creaked open.

"Hey." Luke filled the opening. "I thought you might need a little help." He lifted what was probably twenty sheets of paper towels scrunched in his hands. Some were wet, most were dry.

God I love this man. She closed her eyes, fighting another wave of nausea.

The sound of Luke's footsteps moved closer, and she cracked open her eyes just as he bent down next to her, resting on his haunches. Without saying a word, he used one of the wet paper towels to wipe her face. The coldness of the cloth brought some relief.

"Are you feeling well enough to leave yet?"

"I think so."

Luke helped her out of the stall and over to the sink. He held her wild curls away from her face while she rinsed her mouth. Who knew such a simple gesture could make her feel so treasured?

"Thank you," she said when he handed her a paper towel.

The bathroom door swung open, and a woman pulled up short when she saw them at the sink.

"Can you give us one minute?" Luke said as if he had a right to be in the women's restroom.

The woman backed out without a word.

"Here." Luke handed her a piece of peppermint candy. He had quit smoking, but now popped peppermints throughout the day. "They might help get the bad taste out of your mouth."

Christina quickly placed the sweet treat on her tongue. "Thank you. You take such good care of me," she mumbled and leaned into him. He wrapped his arm around her and guided her toward the door.

"I love you and will always be here to take care of you." He kissed the top of her head and opened the door. "Come on. Let's go home."

The End

If you enjoyed this book by Sharon C. Cooper,
please consider leaving a review on any online book site,
review site, or social media outlet.

ABOUT THE AUTHOR

Award-winning and bestselling author, Sharon C. Cooper, spent 10 years as a sheet metal worker. And while enjoying that unique line of work, she attended college in the evening and obtained her B.A. from Concordia University in Business Management with an emphasis in Communication. Sharon is a romance-a-holic - loving anything that involves romance with a happily-ever-after, whether in books, movies or real life. She writes contemporary romance, as well as romantic suspense and enjoys rainy days, carpet picnics, and peanut butter and jelly sandwiches. When Sharon is not writing or working, she's hanging out with her amazing husband, doing volunteer work or reading a good book (a romance of course). To read more about Sharon and her novels, visit:

Website: http://sharoncooper.net
Facebook:
http://www.facebook.com/AuthorSharonCCooper21?ref=hl
Twitter: https://twitter.com/#!/Sharon_Cooper1
Subscribe to her blog: http://sharonccooper.wordpress.com/
Goodreads:
http://www.goodreads.com/author/show/5823574.Sharon_C
_Cooper

OTHER TITLES BY SHARON C. COOPER:

Jenkins Family Series (Contemporary Romance)
Best Woman for the Job (Short Story Prequel)
Still the Best Woman for the Job (book 1)
All You'll Ever Need (book 2)
Tempting the Artist (book 3)
Negotiating for Love – (book 4) – *Coming Soon*
Seducing the Boss Lady – (book 5) – *Coming Soon*

Reunited Series (Romantic Suspense)
Blue Roses (book 1)
Secret Rendezvous (Prequel to Rendezvous with Danger)
Rendezvous with Danger (book 2)
Truth or Consequences (book 3)
Operation Midnight (book 4) – *Coming soon*
Casino Heat (book 5) – *Coming soon*

Stand Alones
Something New ("Edgy" Sweet Romance)
Legal Seduction
(Harlequin Kimani – Contemporary Romance)
Sin City Temptation
(Harlequin Kimani – Contemporary Romance)
A Dose of Passion
(Harlequin Kimani – Contemporary Romance)
coming October 2015

$ 8.99

Made in the USA
Middletown, DE
28 August 2019